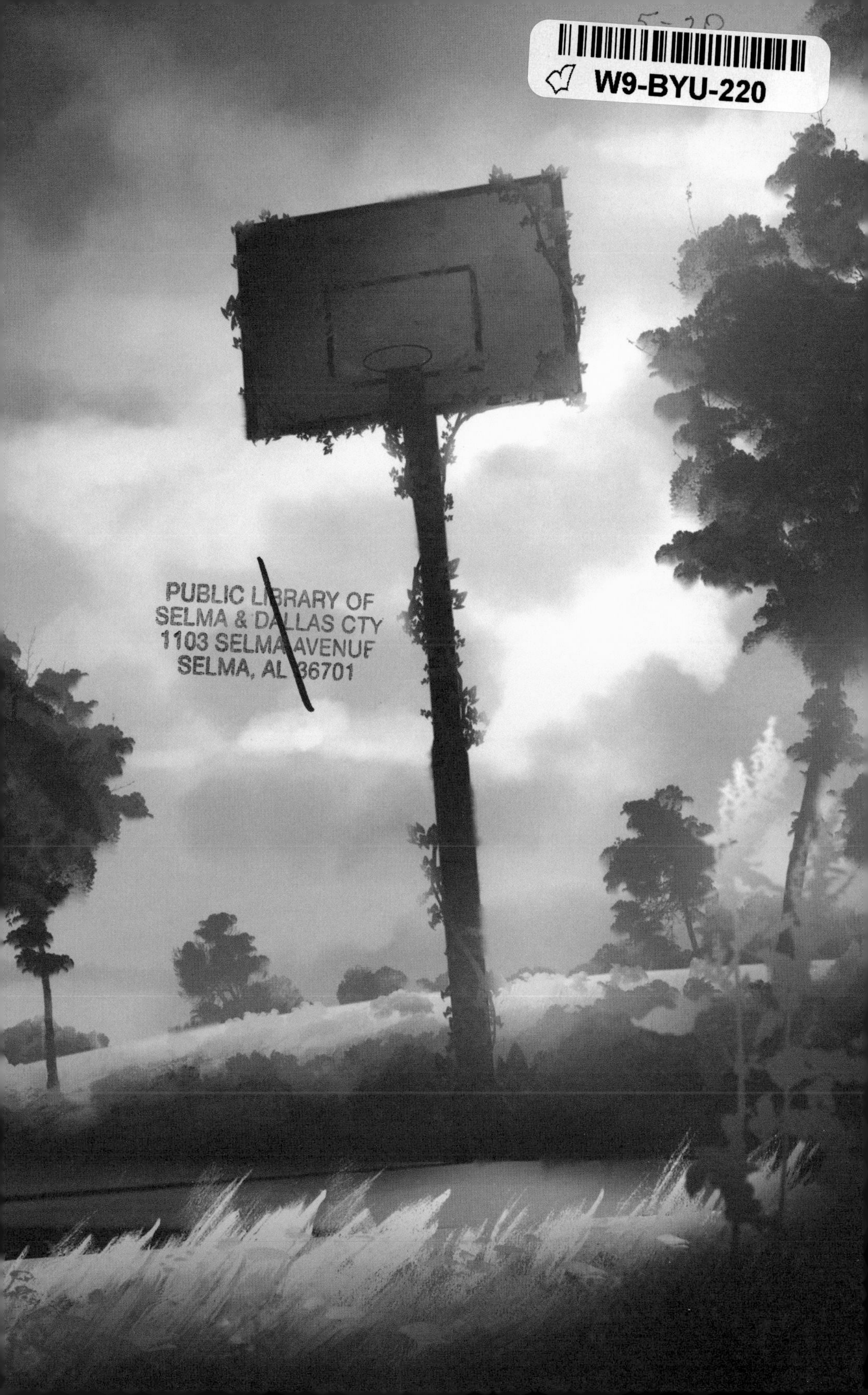

THE WIZENARD SERIES
SEASON ONE

THE WIZENARD SERIES
SEASON ONE

CREATED BY
KOBE BRYANT

WRITTEN BY
WESLEY KING

GRANITY STUDIOS
COSTA MESA, CALIFORNIA

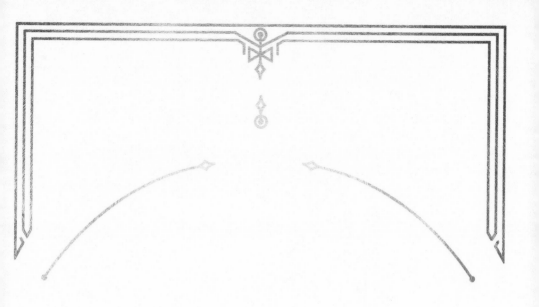

*To young athletes who commit
to doing the hard work.
The process always pays off.*

—KOBE BRYANT

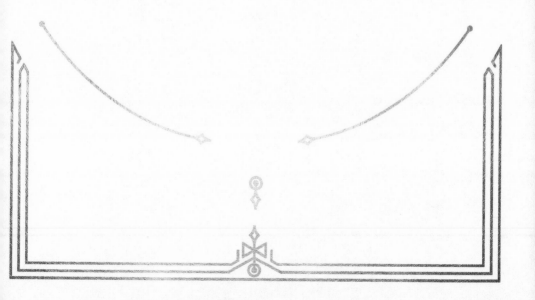

THE WIZENARD SERIES

SEASON ONE

PROLOGUE

Before asking when, tell yourself how.

✦ WIZENARD ◇ 64 ◇ PROVERB ✦

THE BUZZER WENT off, the game ended, and one boy sat alone.

Fairwood was a riot of noise. The visiting team and their fans were laughing and cheering. One spectator had brought a foghorn and was letting it wail like the awakening of some prehistoric monster. But Reginald Mathers and his teammates were quiet. The West Bottom Badgers moved slowly among one another. Curt nods. Sunken shoulders.

It was the first game of a new season, but it felt like an ending.

Reggie looked down at the palms of his hands. Professor Rolabi Wizenard had brought them magic, actual magic, and they had still lost. It seemed as if all the promise of training camp had leached through the polished hardwood floorboards and disappeared forever. Of course it had.

Tonight, Reggie had been promoted to the first sub off the bench, and he had failed spectacularly. He'd played five minutes, maybe, and been terrible the entire time. Turnovers. Missed jumpers. Burned on defense again and again. Reggie had let down the Badgers. Of course he had.

Reggie watched his teammates exchange half-hearted encouragements. Some looked near tears. He stared at his hands again. Reggie felt bad for them. *Them.* That was the word written in the lines of his palms. *Them* instead of *us.*

A minute later, Reggie followed his teammates into the locker room.

"Right back where we started," Twig said softly, breaking the silence.

Reggie's closest friend sounded defeated. Dazed. Reggie felt his stomach aching.

Lab, the Badgers' starting small forward and corner sharpshooter, shook his head. "I thought it was going to be different this year."

"We needed those threes at the end," Peño said, his eyes locked on his younger brother.

Lab scowled. "We needed less turnovers before that—"

"You needed to get a rebound!" Peño shouted. "Not a single second-chance board—"

"Hey!" Rain said, cutting in. "We *all* need to get better before next week. Period."

The room fell into unsettled silence and a few last glares. No one was going to argue with their star player after the incredible game that Rain had just played, but the tension remained. Reggie sensed resentment, and something sharper too.

Professor Rolabi marched into the room, stopped, waited. As ever, he wore his black pin-striped suit, pleats ironed sharp enough to cut butter, and a candy-apple-red bow tie. His strange leather medicine bag hung closed at his side, its secrets locked away. His ice-blue eyes found Reggie.

"We need more from you," Rolabi said. "We need everything from everyone."

The professor stormed out again, and a new silence loomed so heavy that Reggie thought it might flatten him. Twig gave him a sympathetic pat on the knee, but Reggie barely even felt it.

Rolabi had called him out in front of everyone. He had basically *blamed* Reggie.

He vaguely heard the others saying goodbye as they left. Finally, Reggie was alone, still wearing his yellow uniform, and he shuffled out into the empty gym. Someone had turned off all but one row of garish overhead fluorescent panels, which cast just enough light for shadows.

Reggie walked to center court, listening to his footsteps echo in the rafters. His chest felt as hollow as the gym. He had given everything to this sport, and it gave him nothing back. It pushed him away. It rejected him.

Of course it did. He had expected something different this year. He wasn't even sure what exactly . . . but after months of magic and hard work, he thought they could at least *win*.

"Well," Reggie said softly. "It was a nice thought while it lasted."

He didn't even know who he was talking to. Rolabi or Fairwood or grana itself. He supposed it didn't matter. Magic was good for stories, but it didn't belong on a basketball court.

Reggie nodded sadly, fixed his duffel over his shoulder, and headed out into the evening. The Bottom was waiting for him, as it always was.

THE BOY AND HIS BALL

Self-doubt is the beginning of defeat.

✦ WIZENARD ⬥59⬥ PROVERB ✦

ON SATURDAY, REGGIE woke to the smell of coffee, black and strong, wafting in beneath his bedroom door. It was the aroma of Gran's morning. Coffee first, then the sweetness of brown sugar on porridge, and finally a spray of cheap perfume before the clatter of the front door as she left for her shift at the diner.

Six days a week. Ten hours per day. That's what the smell of coffee meant.

Reggie waited until she left, trying to fall back asleep. But his mind was awake and roaming. It was on blown ball games and missed chances and the lies Rolabi Wizenard had told the team. Lies. A harsh word, maybe, but Reggie couldn't think of a better one. The professor had claimed that if they faced their fears, they could beat anyone. He had offered them hope.

Reggie had almost believed it. Twig had shown him that picture book, *The World of Grana*, and it had all seemed so grand

and mystical. The Wizenards had come to save the day. It was a nice story. And that was all.

Reggie rolled over and stared at the sole object perched atop his dresser—a small wooden box without a hinge. The front was engraved with an intricate, hand-carved symbol. His mother had given it to him the year she'd died. She'd told him that she and his father had found it, and that it was very important, and that they wanted Reggie to hold on to it for them and keep it safe. He had dutifully stored it away and only opened it again years after they'd been killed, when he was eleven. While playing around with the box, he had found a false bottom and a note tucked inside.

It read: *He has emptied it. You must fill it. He will try to stop you at all costs.*

Reggie had swiftly tucked it away again, though the thrill of discovery remained. It was the sort of message that heroes found in Gran's old stories. There was even a villain, whoever *he* was. At first, Reggie had no idea what the note meant, or why his parents had left it for him specifically. Over time, though, he'd formed dozens of theories, each more appealing than the last. Intergalactic warriors, dragons and knights, monsters and spies. Then, last summer during training camp, he had landed on an explanation that made so much sense, it had to be true.

Reggie slid his legs off the bed and stood up, stretching his arms over his head and wincing as his fingernails scraped the loose stucco on the ceiling. His bedroom seemed to be shrinking rapidly by the day.

Small as it was, the room had everything Reggie needed: a narrow cot, an old dresser that doubled as a desk—he could remove the lower drawers and slide a stool into the gap—and a coffin-size closet, which was more than sufficient for his meager collection of clothes. Most importantly, he had an empty trash bin in the corner with a backboard drawn on the wall above it in chalk. That bin had been the recipient of a hundred thousand game-winning socks.

Besides, it could have been worse: P had to share the other bedroom with Gran, who snored so loudly, the windows rattled.

Reggie went out to get a drink. Their apartment had four rooms: a bathroom, two small bedrooms, and a larger space that served as kitchen/dining/living room all in one. Butterscotch carpet covered the floors—even in the bathroom—all bordered by soap-green walls dotted with framed photos. They lived in a co-op apartment on Swain Street, infamous as the "Bottom of the Bottom" and widely considered to be the worst neighborhood in the entire country of Dren.

He poured himself some juice and stared out a window, watching the sun crawl over the Bottom cityscape. Shadows fled into narrow alleys or under sagging covered porches. Homes and buildings shed shingles and paint like molting birds. A few cars trundled down the street, most spewing regular puffs of black smoke.

"Heads up!"

He turned as P charged toward him with her ratty old soccer ball at her feet. Reggie's little sister was rarely without the ball—it had been their father's and probably predated even him. The yellowed patches were all worn and sprouting thread, and any logos had long since washed away. The ball was basically a third foot, and as P passed by, she rolled it between Reggie's legs, whooping as she continued toward the fridge.

"A little morning nutmeg for you!" she called over her shoulder.

"Funny."

She poured herself a glass of juice, still rolling the ball around. "Brooding again?"

P was eight years old and had only been one when the accident happened. She looked like Reggie, even if she didn't want to admit it: skinny arms, chicken legs, dark skin, and a broad nose between copper eyes. She even had the same unruly black curls, though P left a few scant inches for braids where Reggie kept his short. Thankfully, she had at least been spared the scar that ran down his chin—Gran said he had taken a fall when he was little and split it open.

"I don't *brood*," he said.

"Is it because you stank yesterday?" P asked.

Reggie rubbed the bridge of his nose. "Remember when we talked about honesty?"

"And how it's always the best policy—"

"No," he cut in. "We said that sometimes you can be *too* honest."

She downed her juice and wiped the orange mustache away. "That does sound familiar."

Reggie sighed. "What are you doing today?"

"Kick around the park for a bit. Then homework so Gran doesn't yell at me. You?"

"Got practice," he said. "Rolabi is probably going to make us run twenty miles."

"Come play soccer instead," she suggested brightly.

"I'll play when you do," he countered.

That was a sore spot, and he knew it. P loved kicking the ball around by herself, but she refused to try out for a team, despite an invitation from the school's coach. Reggie had tried a million times to convince her to go for it, but she flat out refused.

P glared at him, then nutmegged him again on the way to her room. "No thanks."

She disappeared inside, and Reggie stared down at the city again. The morning sun caught the top of a huge bronze statue dominating the intersection at Finney and Loyalist. It was a depiction of a scowling President Talin, turning moss green as it aged, all of it speckled white compliments of the Bottom's many pigeons. He was the second Loyalist Party president since the Split and even worse than his predecessor: Talin had ruled for twenty-nine authoritative years. He was far away in the capital city, Argen, but the statue was a reminder of his watchful eye. Reggie despised that statue more than anything . . . well, except for Talin himself.

He checked the clock over the stove. It was time to start getting ready for practice.

"Well," Reggie said softly. "This should be fun."

Reggie arrived at Fairwood early, as usual. He loved the time before practice. It was quiet and hopeful, and even a bench player like him could shine for a while in an empty sky. There were no cheers for makes, but there were no groans for misses either. It was a fair trade, given his percentages.

Reggie laced up his sneakers, pausing for a moment to run his fingertips along the soft white leather. Gran had bought the shoes for him at the start of the season, and he knew very well what they represented. Hours and hours of overtime at the diner. Old hands worn raw from hot, soapy water and feet blistered from pacing tile floors. His school shoes were the same. His clothes. Everything had been bought with Gran's sweat. And though he loved the white sneakers, guilt seeped in every time he looked at them.

She believed in him. And she was wrong.

Reggie launched into his normal warm-up routine—shooting casual jumpers from around the floor. He only had one rule: he always tried to make five hundred shots a day. He wasn't even sure where the rule had come from, but he was very diligent about following it.

As usual, Reggie began to rack up layups and free throws, the two easiest shots for him to hit. He practiced his form studiously. He tried to shoot like he was standing atop a crumbling mountain. He flicked his wrist. Pointed his toes. Kept his elbow in line with the hoop. He did everything that Rolabi had said.

Twenty minutes and 113 makes in, Reggie hit a turnaround jumper on the post and ran to the free-throw line. He set his feet, dribbled once for focus, and then looked up to shoot.

"Oh no," he murmured.

The hoop was gone. The glass backboard remained, as did the black metal struts stretching down from the ceiling. It was all there . . . except for a rim. Reggie looked around.

"Rolabi?"

He slowly walked under the backboard, then jumped and

swatted, checking whether the mesh was invisible but still there. Nothing. Reggie had seen enough grana at work to know such things were possible. But he had yet to figure out how it worked, or why. In fact, he still knew almost nothing about grana apart from one important fact: it seemed to skip over him.

The other players often spaced out during practices, consumed by their visions. Sometimes they disappeared and returned, then alluded to strange adventures. But not Reggie. He had of course experienced magical things during training camp, in the presence of Rolabi Wizenard and the whole team: the tiger, the castle, the crumbling mountaintop, the collapsing walls of the gym. But on those occasions, he had always assumed he was riding on his teammates' coattails. Grana had otherwise ignored him. That in itself wasn't a surprise.

But why was it showing up for him now?

"I hope you're more useful for everyone else," Reggie grumbled.

He had a flash of hope, turned to the far hoop, and sighed. That one was gone too.

"Figures."

He tried to think back to that picture book about Wizenards and grana that Twig had found. There didn't seem to be anything in there about actually controlling grana. Reggie cleared his throat.

"Well, grana. Magic. Whatever you are. I command you to bring the hoops back."

He waited for a moment.

"Please?" he added hopefully.

But the gym stood silent. There was no flash of magic. There was, of course, nothing.

Just an idiot, a basketball, and nothing to do with it, Reggie thought glumly.

He plunked onto the bench, figuring he would wait for the others to arrive. Grana liked them. Rain would probably get six hoops. Reggie rolled the ball around in his hands, feeling thoroughly miserable. When he looked up, the rims had reappeared. He grinned and started across the floor.

"See, we can get along—" He stopped, nearly at the free-throw line. "Hey!"

They had vanished again.

"This isn't funny!"

Annoyed, he trudged back to the bench. And, once again, the hoops reappeared.

"I get it," he said. "Grana is a big, stupid jerk!"

He flinched and looked up, hoping he wasn't about to get crushed by a falling boulder or something. But as before, Fairwood just stared back at him.

Hoping to calm his churning mind, Reggie started jogging around the perimeter of the court, dribbling as he went. As he rounded a corner, he paused and noticed something odd. The hoop materialized, but only when Reggie stood inside the corner. When he jogged along the sidelines or stepped closer to the hoop, it blinked away again. Reggie continued on, frowning. He tried the next corner, then another. Each time, the closest hoop returned. Did grana want him to shoot corner threes? Was it *that* malicious?

"You asked for it," he muttered, and stopped at the next corner.

Reggie loosened his shoulders, dribbled twice, and set up for the jumper. He wasn't exactly sure why he was so terrible from the corner. A matter of angles, probably. It was supposed to be the easiest three-pointer to make, which only made his endless misses more infuriating. Reggie put up the shot. The ball clanked hard off the front rim and bounced away.

"Happy?" he asked loudly. "I suck at corner threes. I knew that already."

He grabbed his rebound and moved to another spot on the floor . . . but once again, the hoop disappeared.

"Perfect," he said. "Only four hundred makes to go. I'll be here for a month."

Reggie reluctantly started shooting corner threes. The next shot missed left. Then long.

"Just drop!" Reggie shouted after missing a fourth attempt.

He could feel his temper rising. When he ran to the corner and turned back for another attempt, things got worse. The hoop had shrunk to no bigger than the roll of masking tape Gran kept in the linen closet. Reggie rubbed his forehead in exasperation.

He switched to his deepest, most Rolabi-like voice: "Go back to normal size. Now!"

The tiny rim didn't budge. Reggie took the shot, setting his feet and watching the ball arc perfectly toward the waiting hoop . . . where it plunked off the little metal circle and bounced away. He ran after it, thoroughly angry now.

"I thought grana was supposed to help people!"

He retrieved the ball at center court and turned back to the hoop. It was gone again. He stared at the backboard, fuming. Grana had helped his teammates. Naturally, it was taunting him.

"I just want to play ball. We all know I stink. We all know I'm not going anywhere. If you're trying to remind me of that, congratulations. You win. Reggie stinks. Now, are we done?"

He looked around, saw nothing, and then nodded.

"Good. Bring that hoop back right now and we can go on ignoring each other—"

Reggie was cut off as the floor suddenly gave way beneath him. The dot at center court plunged downward, pulling the hardwood planks with it, and his shoes lost all traction and began to slide. He threw himself toward the wall, trying to grab on to something, but he was too late.

With a last, breathless scream, he tumbled into the darkness.

THOSE WHO DARE

A champion turns weakness into strength.

REGGIE SLID DOWN on the pitched hardwood floor, gliding over the wax. Panicked, he rolled onto his stomach, trying to slow his descent. But it was useless. He managed a look over his shoulder and saw that a flat surface was now in view. And it was coming up fast.

He closed his eyes, feeling his body seize as he waited for the inevitable crunch of bones.

But as he slid, he felt the incline begin to change, becoming flatter and flatter until he was lying horizontally again. He opened his eyes, almost warily. He was indeed on flat ground, though that was the only good news. He was lying at the bottom of a massive cone, as if the entire gym had warped into a funnel. It was gently curved into a bowl at the base of the cone, which at least explained why he wasn't a Reggie-shaped splatter.

Towering hardwood walls rose around him, smooth and

growing steeper toward the top, surrounding this flat space about the size of his bedroom. Thin, weak light trickled down from the gym's fluorescent panels, now distant overhead. Slowly climbing to his feet, Reggie saw the two hoops leaning over the edge way above him—little more than two orange specks from his vantage point. He was thoroughly trapped.

"This is great," Reggie murmured.

He tried to think. His beloved basketball had fallen in with him and now sat loyally by his feet, though he wasn't sure what possible good it would do.

Reggie began to pace around his ball, staring up at the distant hoops.

"Okay," he said. "Grana didn't kill me—yet—so this must be a test." He rubbed his forehead, scowling. "Of course, it did drop me into a giant fifty-foot hole to starve—"

Reggie caught himself, trying not to lose his temper. If he was going to talk to grana, he might as well be polite. Things had been going steadily downhill since he had called it stupid. *Ha*, he thought. *Downhill. Very punny. Twig would have liked that one.* Twig. The team!

Practice was due to start pretty soon. Surely, they would rescue him.

"Hello!" he called. "Guys! Rolabi! Kallo?"

He knew he was feeling desperate if he was hoping for rescue-by-tiger. But though his voice was amplified a thousand times through the giant loudspeaker of the cone, there was no response. Just tiny distant hoops and tiny distant lights and a very long, impossibly steep climb to reach them. What if no one came? What if he was trapped down here forever? What if he could never leave? Reggie felt his throat clamping up. His knees wobbled.

"You can figure this out," he muttered. "It's a puzzle." During training camp, the walls of the gym had almost crushed the entire team, but the Badgers had stopped their terrifying advance by working together. There had to be something Reggie could do now too. "This is easy . . . I just need to . . . score a very long-range three-pointer?"

He looked up. It seemed unlikely—actually, impossible—but he picked up the ball, cocked it back, and tried to heave it toward one of the hoops with all his strength. It flew about a third of the way up, lost momentum, and then began racing back down again, ricocheting off the hardwood cliffs.

Without thinking, Reggie tried to catch it. He stepped onto the sloped wall, toppled forward, and then slid back down with a pitiful sigh as the ball eventually settled beside him.

"Okay, so not a three-pointer," he said.

He stood up again and began to pace. It had to be a fundamental basketball skill.

"I could pass it to myself . . . No . . . I'm going to dribble so hard that the floor rises . . . That doesn't even make any sense . . . Okay, I simply box out whenever the ball comes back . . . and . . ."

Reggie sighed. There was no lesson here. Well, maybe one, but he already knew that.

Reggie was right where he belonged.

"Boy at the bottom," he said, sitting cross-legged on the floor. "Good one."

He sat there for a long time. Actually, he wasn't sure if it was ten minutes or ten hours. He stared at the basketball across from him and realized that he probably wasn't capable of getting out of this pit. It should have been scary. Instead, he just felt numb, the way he felt at the end of every game he'd ever lost.

"Fine," he said softly. "This is impossible. So I surrender. You win, grana, whatever you are."

Reggie closed his eyes. When he opened them, he was on level ground at center court. Fairwood appeared to be back to normal. He gingerly stood, scooping up the ball. Hopefully, grana had heard his surrender and given up on him for good.

So why are you here? a voice in his head asked him. *Why come early to every practice?*

Reggie shooed the voice away. *His* voice, though perhaps some rebellious offshoot.

"Thanks for nothing," Reggie said aloud. "Let's just go our own ways."

"You talking to the gym?"

He jumped and then spotted Rain by the front doors, smirking.

"Sort of," Reggie said sheepishly.

Rain laughed and started for the bench. "You ain't the first one, bro."

"What do you say to it?"

"I tell it to watch closely," Rain replied, taking a seat. "I tell it big things are coming."

Reggie smiled and went to go shoot around. He envied Rain. He envied his talent and his athleticism, but mostly, he envied Rain's easy confidence. He *belonged* out on the court. Rain loved ball, just like Reggie. The important difference was that ball seemed to love Rain back.

The warm-up only reinforced that belief. The hoop was still only visible when Reggie went to the corners—and yet Rain shot from anywhere. Sometimes it shrank for Reggie, but whenever Reggie's errant shots bounced off orange iron, it quickly grew again, and Rain swished it easily.

At one point, Reggie sprinted to the corner and saw that the hoop was mercifully a normal size. But in his haste to shoot before it changed again, he misfired completely and airballed it. His cheeks burned.

"You need to take that shot more often," Rain said, popping another turnaround jumper.

Reggie grabbed his rebound and snorted. "You sure about that?"

"Yeah, man. The corner is big for us. You have the right form. It will fall eventually."

"Doesn't seem like it."

Rain stepped up to the corner and drained a three on his first attempt. "It will."

Reggie held back a sigh. And then he missed his next attempt. And another. Rain had the decency to pretend not to notice, and even better, to not say anything when Reggie finally hit one eleven tries later—well past the point of congratulations.

While he was shooting, the rest of the Badgers filed in, and the court was soon crowded. Reggie tried to join them for free throws or layups, hoping their grana would overwhelm his useless, possibly sadistic version, but no such luck. He could either shoot corner threes or he could sit miserably on the bench and watch his teammates shoot from anywhere they wanted. But no one else seemed to notice the constantly changing rim apart from Reggie.

As Reggie shuffled back to the nearest corner, Twig appeared beside him.

"You look bummed," Twig said, hitting a turnaround jumper.

Reggie paused. "I've . . . been in a bit of a hole today."

"I would say that was a metaphor, but you never know these days. What happened?"

"Don't even ask," Reggie said, prepping for another shot.

"So you did fall in a hole?"

Reggie sighed. "What did I just say?"

"Fine, fine. Well, we lost again. And I really thought we were going to wizenard them."

"You're using *wizenard* as a verb now?" Reggie said.

"Why not?" Twig pumped his fist. "Let's get out there and wizenard those guys—"

"That doesn't even make sense."

"Fine. Can we grana someone, then? I mean, admittedly I was kind of hoping that we were going to have superpowers or something when the game started. Like a ten-foot vertical or stretchy arms. Or, you know, a win, at least."

"Yeah," Reggie said, eyeing the hoop. "Grana didn't seem to be any advantage at all."

Twig patted Reggie's shoulder, perhaps sensing how down he felt. "It's just one game."

"Just like all the others," Reggie mumbled.

Reggie put up another three, and the net seemingly *moved* out of the way, letting it sail right past. They watched together as

Reggie's errant shot bounced off the wall and under the bleachers.

"Are you seeing anything when I shoot the ball?" Reggie asked, frustrated.

"Well . . . like an air ball?"

"No. Like the rim moving. Shrinking, disappearing—"

Twig shrugged. "I told you already. I think we can only see our own grana stuff. I've never seen anyone else's. Why . . . have you?"

Reggie glanced down the court and saw a Hula-Hoop rim waiting for Rain.

"Sometimes," he admitted.

Twig stepped closer. "Really? Dude, why didn't you tell me—"

"It's not a big deal. Just little glimpses."

Twig flushed. "Did you see anything around me? Reflections?"

"No. I just see the hoops moving and sometimes the floor. What reflections?"

"Nothing." Twig shook his head. "I wish Rolabi would tell us more about grana. I mean, he's a Wizenard. Oh . . . that reminds me. I checked another library for Wizenard info."

They had agreed that Twig would check his libraries in the nicer north end; there were no libraries left in the West Bottom, apart from the one at school, and Reggie had long since combed through that. They did have internet in the Bottom, though it was down more often than not, and always spotty. Twig had tried that on their behalf too, but he said search results were blocked for grana, Wizenards . . . everything. Books had been their best bet.

"And?"

"Nothing."

Reggie sighed and started for his ball. He had read a little bit about the Split that happened decades before Reggie was born—the nickname for the Loyalist Party's takeover and their subsequent closing of Dren's borders. All "dangerous" information from the outside world had been destroyed, supposedly to protect the population.

"I told you that. The Loyalists would have been thorough—"

"*Except* for a little book I found sandwiched between two shelves. Come on."

"You . . . what?"

Reggie quickly followed him to the bench, where Twig withdrew from his bag a small leather-bound book, so old and cracked, it looked like it was shedding. The cover had a strange symbol with four distinct segments and a looping hand-drawn title: *The Cosmological Connectivity of Spiritual Resonance and Transmutation.*

Reggie glanced up at him, raising an eyebrow. "Rolls off the tongue. What does this have to do with—"

"Just flip through."

Reggie did as he was told. The book was speckled with unusual illustrations: pencil-shaded designs of "emotion machines" and "energy-storage vats" alongside elaborate watercolor symbols that seemed to represent the full spectrum of human emotion—all in incredible detail.

"Twig—"

"Almost there."

Reggie kept flipping, and finally, he saw a chapter titled "The Origin of Grana." He looked up at a smiling Twig and then went back to flipping pages. The emotional resonance of grana in humanity. The peaks and pitfalls of hope. He flipped again, and his breath caught in his throat.

"What is it?" Twig asked, frowning.

There was a lone symbol dominating the page—one he had stared at for years.

Below the symbol, the caption read: *The Amplification of Emotional Strength.*

"Can I borrow this for a day or two?" Reggie managed, barely able to speak.

Twig watched him for a moment, clearly wanting to ask more. Then he just nodded.

"Sure."

Reggie tucked the book into his bag, thought of something, and then grabbed Twig's arm.

"You better not check out any more books about grana—" Reggie started.

Twig nodded. "This book didn't even have a code anymore. I just took it."

"Good. I am positive Talin and his cronies got rid of these for a reason. He doesn't want people reading about grana. I have no idea why, since it seems intent on making our lives more difficult, if anything, but they wiped it all away for a reason. They wanted Dren to forget."

He was speculating, of course, but it had all begun to make sense. His parents, their criticism of the government, the fact that all traces of grana had been wiped away . . . it all pointed back to Talin. He and Twig had been sharing theories for weeks. Of course, if Talin was behind it all, and if he *was* trying to remove all traces of grana, then the Badgers had to be very careful.

No one could find out they were using grana.

"I know," Twig said. "Unfortunately for him, he forgot about Rolabi Wizenard."

As if on cue, a gust of wind swept across the gym, bitter cold and carrying the fresh scent of salt and sand, like a beach wreathed in snow. The doors burst open, and Rolabi strode onto the court.

"Gather round."

Reggie and Twig exchanged a knowing look, then joined the others in front of the professor.

As Reggie approached, the professor turned to him, his eyes flashing sea green.

"What does the storm say to the mountain?" he asked.

The rest of the Badgers turned to Reggie as well, perhaps expecting him to have an answer. Reggie's mouth worked, but no sound came out. He had no idea, and he was far too stunned to speak anyway. Rolabi almost sounded *angry* with him. It was absolutely terrifying.

"I don't know," Reggie finally managed.

"It says: *Bend.* And the mountain replies: *Break.* And so the storm flees the mountain."

Reggie stared up at the professor. "I don't understand."

"I know. Twenty laps, then free throws. Five more for every miss. Reggie shoots first."

The team groaned and ran for the sidelines, jostling into a teardrop shape.

Reggie started after the others, then glanced back. "Sir, if I did something wrong—"

"You did," Rolabi replied curtly. "But not to me."

Reggie wanted to ask more, but the look on the professor's face sent him scurrying after the others. *Maybe I shouldn't have called grana stupid*, he thought glumly. *He probably heard.*

He still wasn't exactly sure just how powerful Rolabi was—the picture book described Wizenards as teachers, but it didn't get into much more detail. Sometimes it seemed like the professor knew about everything happening in Fairwood, whether he was there or not. Was he a scholar of grana . . . or more of a sorcerer? Whatever he was, he didn't seem very happy with Reggie.

Twenty laps in, Reggie made his way to the free-throw line. Feeling the eyes of his teammates on him, he missed, and the Badgers set off on five more laps. Rain moved to shoot next, but Rolabi shook his head and pointed wordlessly at Reggie. Reggie flushed, stepped up to the line, and missed again. His ears burned at his teammates' groans and mutters as they broke into another run.

Mercifully, Reggie hit his third attempt and then quickly melted back into the group, ashamed at the attention. Ashamed, but also agitated. Why did Rolabi have to call him out like that? Reggie worked just as hard as everyone else did. He tried to shake it off. It was probably just a quick reprimand. He *had* stunk out on the court last night, in fairness, and right after Rolabi had named him the unofficial "sixth man."

But, as it turned out, the free throws were just the beginning of a very long practice.

The professor stayed close to him during the drills, pointing out Reggie's errors. On defense, he sent Reggie to guard Rain off of screen plays, or Cash in the low post, or Peño in the open floor. Reggie was outmatched in every position and beat again and again.

Reggie was crossed over and bodied hard and scored on. He fumed but said nothing. Whenever Reggie turned the ball over, Rolabi had them run. When Reggie missed a shot, Rolabi had them run. When Reggie *didn't* collect a rebound or make a stop on defense, he had them all run.

Two hours later—Reggie was thoroughly humiliated by then—Rolabi called them in.

"I am your coach," he said, "not your motivator. My job is not to tell you how hard to work. Or why you should. That is your job. Take a good look at yourselves this week. Either you want to be the best player you can be . . . or you don't. It's your choice. You alone know if you have the desire and the strength to reach your full potential. Be honest. Because only you can motivate yourself."

He gestured to the bench, dismissing them.

"I'll see you Monday night."

Reggie stalked right past Rolabi, pointedly not making eye contact with him.

"Make your choice, Reggie," the professor said. "And do it soon."

Then he left, the doors bursting open before him and thundering shut, propelled by another arctic gust. Reggie furiously changed into his boots and walked home, hands balled into fists.

"Choice?" he muttered. "What choice do I have? I show up, don't I? I'm trying."

Raindrops suddenly broke from the sky—and thickened into a cold, bracing sheet of sulfurous smog-water. Reggie put his head down and started running, splashing through puddles. A chill seeped through his clothes in an instant and made its way down into his bones. He pumped his legs harder, trying to outrun the rain.

When he finally got home, soaked and exhausted, he managed a quick change of clothes and face-planted into bed. He lay there for a moment, then reached out and grabbed the old box.

He ran his fingers over the symbol, then retrieved the book as well. There was no doubting it: the symbol was the same. And if the book was about grana, then his box must have something to do with grana too. Which meant his parents might have known about grana. He felt his skin prickling. If they knew about grana, then it made even more sense that they were silenced . . . Had they experienced it too? Had they had visions like him? Had they met a Wizenard?

Reggie took a deep breath and started to read.

"The amplification of emotional strength," he read aloud. "Part One. The Subject."

He read the chapter three times, and at the end of it, he still had no idea what it meant. It was all vague words and cryptic illustrations. The labels and descriptions seemed to make no sense at all: *the amalgamation of misery* and *super-succession* and the bolded word *Muse* stamped into the collected center of a colorful petal-like symbol that grew with every page. It was complete nonsense, and, more importantly, it gave no hint as to why his mother had given him the box.

Reggie lay back on the bed and sighed deeply. Maybe it was all just a coincidence.

He thought of the first line of the chapter: *The subject is not always one who is expected. Greatness can be fostered from any source, if only they can bear the elements, if only they dare.*

He wasn't sure what the "subject" was, or what elements the writer was referring to, but his eyes naturally lingered on the second line: "Greatness can be fostered from any source."

"I guess that could be me," Reggie said hopefully.

But deep down, he knew it wasn't. He thought of his parents, and how they might have known about grana. Maybe they were watching over him now, urging him to keep going, to figure it out. The thought was comforting for a moment, but as always, it soon trickled away, leaving only loneliness. He didn't want to guess what amazing things they saw or didn't see. He wanted to ask. He just wished that they were here.

Reggie put the book away and lay down, staring up at the stucco.

He had learned a long time ago that wishing didn't work.

SLEEPLESS DREAMS

Every human is born to change the world.
Unfortunately, some are changed by the world first.

✧ WIZENARD ◈55◈ PROVERB ✧

REGGIE SPUN BACK, leaping off his right foot into a dramatic fadeaway jumper.

"Three . . . two . . . onnnnnnne . . ."

The sock hit the wastebasket's lid and bounced out.

"And they miss the playoffs again," Reggie finished, slouching. "The Badgers still stink."

"Gran wants to know if you require a formal invitation to dinner."

He sighed and glanced at P in the doorway. "Coming."

Gran was seated at the head of the kitchen table, a squat wooden circle sandwiched between counter and couch. She was a small woman: five foot three and a hundred pounds, maybe, but she'd never seemed small—even now that he towered over her wispy shock of hair. She filled the room. She rarely got angry and never yelled, and she never needed to—one look was enough.

"Ready to eat, Your Majesty?" Gran asked dryly.

"Sorry," Reggie mumbled.

It was chicken and grits today, with some precious spinach at the side. Vegetables were expensive in the Bottom, but Gran was diligent. She insisted that they eat right, as best they could.

"You've been moping since I got home," Gran said. "Was practice that bad?"

"Yeah," he said quietly.

"Well, that Rolabi knows what he is doing. P, eat, child."

P groaned and took a bite.

"Is your homework done?" Gran asked, eyes flicking back and forth between them.

"It's Saturday," P said.

He could hear her rolling the soccer ball around beneath the table. She had a scavenged newspaper in front of her, open as always to the sports section and the soccer statistics of Dren's professional league. She studied them constantly, and could recite every player's season totals.

"And?" Gran said.

Reggie snorted. "Mine is done."

"So is mine, *obviously*," P said. "So . . . can I hang out at the park tomorrow?"

"Sunday is chore day," Gran reminded her.

P groaned again. "Every day is chore day."

"Right you are," Gran said. "So, what was so bad about practice, Reggie?"

Reggie thought back to practice and felt his stomach turn.

Where to even start? Why was Rolabi being so hard on him all of a sudden? And what did that weird story about the mountain mean? Why would it say "break" to a storm? Reggie put his fork down, his appetite firmly gone.

"It was fine," he said.

Gran stared at him as she chewed, her small, dark eyes locked on his.

"You just keep practicing," she said. "You'll get there."

"I'm not going anywhere, Gran."

"It takes time—"

"It's not about time," Reggie said curtly. "I just don't have it. Period. Can we drop it?"

"Well, I believe in you—"

"Then *stop*," Reggie cut in, feeling the heat in his cheeks. "Can I be excused?"

She stared at him for a moment longer, the muscles twitching in her cheeks. "Fine."

Reggie went to his room and lay down, dejected. He felt guilty for snapping at Gran, but even worse for disappointing her. He tried to push the thought away. He just had to get better. Of course, that was proving more difficult by the day. Why was grana against him?

And even more importantly: How could he fix it?

Reggie woke to darkness, as he often did. He slept little and slept well almost never. Sometimes dreams woke him. Sometimes dreams didn't let him sleep at all.

He turned to his alarm clock and groaned: 3:00 a.m. He'd slept right through the evening—nearly eight hours already. It was the longest he'd slept in months.

Reggie threw aside his blanket, fished around in his dresser, and pulled out an old, rolled-up sock. Easing his way across the room, he began to shoot, whispering the commentary this time.

"Reggie goes left," he said softly, "eyes down the court. He pulls up and—"

"Goes to sleep."

He turned and saw Gran standing in the open doorway, arms folded.

"No wonder you are awake after such an early bedtime."

"Did I wake you?"

"You did. Winning championships past midnight again, I see?"

He flushed. "Maybe."

She walked in and sat on his bed, looking at the old box. "You've been up in the night shooting socks as long as I can remember. Playing ball is all you've ever wanted to do."

"Yeah." He retrieved the sock and sat down beside her. "Too bad I'm better with a sock than a real ball."

She snorted. "Lots of practice. Facing a little easier defense in here too."

"I think it's the dramatic commentary."

"Maybe so." She glanced at him. "I'm worried about you, Reggie."

"I think a lot of kids talk to themselves, Gran—"

"Not about that," she said, rolling her eyes. "In general. You're getting worse."

"At basketball?" Reggie asked, frowning.

"No. At isolating yourself. You don't hang out with anyone outside of school or basketball. You space out every dinner. You lock yourself in your room. You cradle that box—"

"I think 'cradle' is a strong word," Reggie muttered.

"And you don't sleep. I know you miss them. So do I. But you have to move on."

Reggie followed her eyes to the wooden box. He had asked her about it many times, including the cryptic note, but she said she had no idea. "I have. They died almost seven years ago."

"Not for you. For you it's like it was yesterday. I know you want to blame Talin—"

Blood rushed to his cheeks. "I'm going to prove it—"

"And nothing I say seems to dissuade you," she cut in gently. "But I will say it again . . . it is dangerous to go digging for information. Even here. You need to accept what happened, Reg."

Reggie looked away. "I have. And I still think you're not telling me everything."

"Reggie . . ."

"Where did they die? What happened to the car? Where were they going?"

"Reggie, this doesn't help you—"

"Neither does lying." He caught himself and glanced at her. "Sorry."

But Gran didn't flash one of her infamous looks. She just sighed. "I have tried to help you move on. You insist on looking for more, and that's what keeps the old wound open, Reggie. It is festering. And you grow sick with it."

They were silent for a long moment. Reggie felt pressure behind his eyes, but he held it in. He didn't want Gran to see the truth in her words. It did claw at him. But he couldn't move on.

They deserved more. They deserved answers.

"I'm fine," Reggie said.

"Saying that doesn't make it so, Reggie. No matter how many times you say it."

"I am fine," he replied stubbornly.

Gran sighed deeply, patted his hand, and started for the door.

"Get some sleep, Reggie. You can win some more championships in the morning."

That got a reluctant smile from him, and she returned it and gently closed the door.

Reggie climbed into bed. He lay there for hours, thinking of his parents and eventually, as always, of the man who had taken them. Reggie didn't know for sure yet, of course, but he had the note, he had their old articles criticizing the government, and more than that, he just knew it in his gut. He *knew* Talin had ordered their deaths to silence them. And now, he knew that grana may have played a part in that too. Gran was wrong. He needed to uncover the truth.

Talin's pale face seemed to hang in the darkness, smiling as if taunting him.

Reggie didn't sleep until the first light of morning crept under his doorway.

GRANA GAMES

When the road grows hard, and your legs tire,
know that greatness lies ahead.

◆ WIZENARD ◇51◇ PROVERB ◆

ON THURSDAY EVENING, Reggie was out the door two hours before practice as always, galloping down seven stories of scuffed concrete steps and out into the evening sunlight. It was damp and cool, so he pulled his hoodie drawstrings tight and broke into a jog, duffel smacking off his back like a pendulum. He ran right past the bus stop. Reggie wanted to run, to feel the fire in his legs.

School had been uneventful the last few days. As usual, he put his head down in class and did his work. Most of his teammates went to his school, but he wasn't overly close with anyone apart from Twig, who lived way up in the north end. Rain was often busy being fawned over, and Peño was usually in the thick of the crowd, with the rest of the team swirling around the two of them . . . all but Reggie. He kept quiet and still, and when he left school after the last bell, he wanted to *move*.

As he passed by the towering statue of President Talin, he

stopped, staring up at the pointed nose and sallow cheeks and bronze eyes that captured the cold, dead stare in his twice-a-year addresses to the nation. Reggie could almost hear the rasping voice to accompany it.

He could have taken a different route and avoided the statue. But whenever he walked, he felt compelled to come this way. To remember what had happened to his parents, and who he believed had done it. It was likely as close to Talin as he would ever get. His minions might pass through, but Talin himself would never step foot in the Bottom. Reggie would never get to see his cruel smile in person.

Well, unless they got to nationals. He shook his head and kept walking. Not very likely.

Reggie jogged the entire way to Fairwood, shoes pounding over the cracked concrete parking lot last of all, where weeds ringed the curbs and the West Bottom's last tree stood sentry.

As always, Reggie tentatively reached for the door, hoping it would be unlocked, and then grinned when it swung open. He recalled when Fairwood used to drape visitors with a muggy blanket of dust on entry. Now the air was cool and dry, and it smelled like fresh wax instead of a hundred years of accumulated sock sweat. Reggie laughed when the panels flicked on.

"Thanks," he said. "Does this mean we're going to be friends today?"

Reggie pulled on his sneakers and began to dribble between his legs for a warm-up, letting blood flow to his muscles like oil to a piston. He went to shoot from the free-throw line, hoping to get a few buckets and build a little confidence. He needed it after Friday. But, of course, the gym still wouldn't allow it. The hoop appeared only when he traipsed back into the corner.

"Guess not," he muttered.

As he began to shoot around, he noticed it wasn't just the corner today—he could also see the hoop from the dreaded mid-range two as well. But those were the only spots. Five hundred makes, and he had to hit them all from his worst spots on the floor. Sighing, Reggie got to work, watching glumly as one shot after another clanked off iron, or worse, missed altogether.

"Still not sure how this is helping me," he said.

At one point, Reggie glanced at the far hoop and saw that it was still there. Desperate, he decided to try for some layups. Reggie sprinted for the hoop, but with every step, the court seemed to expand by ten feet. By half-court, the hoop was a mile away and receding ever farther.

"Can I just play basketball?" Reggie shouted.

Reggie turned back the way he had come and cried out in frustration. Now the first hoop was a mile off too.

"Fine!" he said. "You want me to run? I can run."

Reggie started his dribble again, heading back for the original hoop. The minutes stretched as he ran. Soon, it felt like hours.

Halfway there, the floor tilted upward at a 45-degree angle, until he was struggling for every step, his thighs and quads burning. To add to the misery, the floor became sticky like fresh concrete, pulling at his soles. Even the heat seemed to build, until he felt like he was more sweat than skin. Reggie's feet began to drag along the clinging hardwood, and soon, he was shuffling and grimacing and stepping on his own tired, clumsy feet.

Finally, Reggie stepped on a dangling lace and toppled forward, face-first.

Reggie lay there for a long moment, exhausted. Then he slowly pushed himself up onto his knees. He saw that the gym was back to normal, and that his ball had rolled out of his grasp when he fell and stopped right beside the bench. Reggie pushed himself up, nodding.

"Yeah, I belong on the bench," he said. "You don't have to rub it in."

He sat on the bench, wiped his forehead with his sleeve, and stared forlornly at the empty court. The hoops had returned, of course. Grana was definitely mocking him.

He tried to wait for the others, but eventually, his need to play won out. The urge was always there. It was waiting when he woke up, tugging at him when he went to sleep. Some nameless, faceless desire that lived deep down in his bones. It brought him here early. It made him leave late.

A natural need without natural talent. A combination good only for heartbreak.

Reggie stood up again, dribbled toward the rim, and allowed a smile when it didn't blink out of existence as he approached. Maybe grana was finally going to cut him some slack.

"Reggie Mathers coming off the high screen. The clock is running." Reggie picked up his pace, crossing over to his left hand and heading for the paint. "He's around another defender now. Whoa, does this kid have handles. Three, two—he drives for the hoop—"

Reggie leapt from the foul line, stretching out for the one-handed floater, grinning right until a night-black shadow swept across his path and swatted the ball straight into the stands. Reggie landed awkwardly, barely staying on his feet. The shadow gestured for him to retrieve the ball.

"I want to play alone today," Reggie said, annoyed. "I just want to *play* period."

The shadow stared at him.

"Right. No mouth, no talking."

Reggie scooped up the ball and dribbled to the top of the key, eyeing the waiting shadow. He had seen the shadow many times after its first appearance back in training camp. It was a perfect three-dimensional silhouette of himself, with much more substance than an ordinary shadow. Its hits and blocks were as solid as anybody's—or harder, as if it was defending the hoop with liquid concrete rather than flesh and muscle. As Reggie approached, the shadow beckoned him with an upraised hand.

Reggie began to dribble, weighing his options, then charged to his right. Before he could even try a shot, his shadow leapt forward and collided with his chest, knocking him back.

"Really?" Reggie said. "You don't think that was a foul?"

Reggie grabbed the ball and charged again, sidestepping the defender and trying to force it down the lane. Once again, he didn't make it. His shadow smacked his wrist, and the ball rolled free. Reggie whirled on his opponent, glaring, but the faceless shadow held its ground, apparently unmoved.

"Fine," Reggie snarled. "That's fine. I can take a few fouls."

Reggie grabbed the ball and faked another direct drive. But

halfway into the lane, he stopped, pulled up for a jumper . . . and was promptly elbowed in the sternum. He doubled over.

"Come on!" Reggie shouted. "This isn't even basketball."

Naturally, his shadow didn't respond. Reggie growled and attacked again.

It didn't go well. His shadow stopped every attempt—sometimes cleanly and often not. The shadow wasn't Reggie's only challenge either. Fairwood seemed to be conspiring against him: the floor slanted upward, the hoop disappeared, the floorboards stuck. Sometimes an invisible wall forced Reggie back toward the defender, even when he had a clear opening the other way.

At one point, he tried to catch his breath, dribbling the ball at the top of the arc. Then his hands began to tingle. Then sting. He looked down and yelped. The ball had caught fire—rippling orange and red flames tinged with emerald green. He panicked and tossed a wild three-pointer, watching dejectedly as it missed both hoop and backboard and hit the far wall.

The next play he went for a layup, and his hand was slapped, jarring the ball loose.

"Come on!" Reggie shouted. "Foul!"

Reggie retrieved the ball and turned back to the hoop . . . and his nose promptly smacked off a wall. No. The *floor*. The hardwood now ran straight up on a 90-degree angle, and the hoop was leaning out overhead. His shadow stood on the vertical floor as well, clearly unbothered by the physics. In fact, it just beckoned for him to attack again.

Reggie fell to his knees, letting the ball roll away. It was impossible. He would have to fly to get to the hoop, and he was so tired, he could barely walk. Reggie pressed his forehead against the hardwood wall and felt sweat trickle along his jaw.

"Why does this game hate me?" he whispered.

With a soft creaking of wood, the walls and floor returned to their usual positions. A second later, the front doors burst open. Twig, Peño, and Lab walked in, talking and filling the gym with laughter. Reggie stood up, forcing a smile.

Peño nodded. "What up, Reg?"

"Nothing," Reggie said quickly. "Just shooting around."

"Well, hopefully you're saving some buckets for tomorrow," Lab said. "We need them."

Peño and Lab went to the bench to change their shoes, while Twig walked over and gave Reggie props.

"Ready for another day of craziness?" Twig asked.

"Always," Reggie said shakily, meeting Twig's bony knuckles with his own.

"You good?"

"Yeah. I'm fine."

Reggie recalled Gran's words and tried to shake them away. He was fine. He had to be.

Twig eyed him suspiciously. "Was it a grana vision—"

"Reggie!" Peño called, interrupting. "I've been thinking of a new nickname for you."

Reggie sighed, though he was happy for the distraction. Twig was still watching him suspiciously, checking around the gym as well for any signs of danger.

"Not again," Reggie said.

"It's just unequal. Yours is just a short form . . . not a nick-name. I mean, he's *Twig*."

"He hated his nickname," Reggie protested.

"I like it now," Twig said. "Was it another hole—"

"And there's Rain," Peño continued, "me, of course, and Lab, and Cash—"

"And Vin, Jerome, me . . ." Reggie said. "They have short-form names too."

Peño waved a hand in dismissal. "I'm working on those. So, listen, here's what I've got so far. You ready?"

"No," Reggie said.

Twig was already snickering beside him.

"Perfect," Peño replied, ignoring him. "Okay, so . . . and give it a chance . . . the Scarecrow."

Reggie stared at him. "The what?"

"Well, you're skinny, and you have a scary look sometimes—see—and . . . okay, fine."

"Was that it?" Reggie asked, starting after his ball.

"Of course not! The Crane? Like the bird? I know we don't have them, but I saw a documentary and . . . Okay, fine. Buckets? Honeybee? Like a Badger. Well, I thought that was good. Okay, here it comes. You're going to love this. Check it out: Reggo-saurus Rex."

Reggie turned back to him, not even bothering to respond.

Peño sighed. "I'm going to go get changed now."

"Good call," Reggie said, biting back a smile.

"You sure you're good?" Twig asked a last time.

Reggie gave him props again. "I'm fine."

He thought of his gran's words: *Saying that doesn't make it so, no matter how many times you say it.* Sometimes he thought Gran knew more about him than he did.

Twig hurried off, and Reggie tried to fall back into his usual shooting routine. As before, the rim was only there from the corners and the mid-range twos. He wanted to scream as one shot after another missed. Once again, he would have to stay well after practice to get his five hundred makes.

When the entire team had arrived, Rolabi started them with laps. As ever when the whole group was together, they all experienced the same visions: running up and down hills, leaping across ever-expanding holes, climbing over rising hardwood walls . . . but sometimes he saw strange things happen to one player only. Cash would have to break through a barrier. Peño would have to jump for a high ladder. But whenever he asked Twig about it, the answer was the same: he couldn't see it.

So why was Reggie able to see everyone else's grana? And if he had that extra ability, why was his own grana so . . . useless?

After the laps, they went straight into an equally tiring runthrough of their systems. On defense, they moved between man and eleven different zones. On attack, there were seemingly endless variations of the Spotlight Offense to be used in any given scenario. It was a lot to remember, but Reggie had them all memorized . . . for *all* positions.

And as with the last practice, Rolabi stayed right on Reggie. He made Reggie demonstrate every difficult play. He told Reggie to lead off each drill without instruction. He loudly explained every single mistake. Reggie held his tongue and worked. He ran. He kept up with everyone else. It still wasn't enough for the professor. The gym shook with his lectures.

"If we play defense without our hands ready, we are tigers without claws."

"Every basket from an offensive rebound is worth ten points. Giving up the rebound is a failure of position."

"Miss one more layup and you will take a hundred after practice."

When practice finally finished, Reggie sat at the end of the bench, waiting for the others to leave. He felt a weight sitting on his shoulders. Grana had given up on him. Rolabi had clearly given up on him too. In fairness, *he* had given up on himself. But, for all that, their season continued tomorrow night. It was another game. Another chance. It was unlikely, but there *was* a chance.

Maybe he could finally make this one count.

THE EAGLES

*If you are fully present in every moment,
time will be your ally.*

❖ WIZENARD ◈53◈ PROVERB ❖

THE EGLINTON EAGLES stalked into Fairwood Community Center like grim sentinels. They wore matching blue-and-white tracksuits, matching chalk-white shoes, and even matching closely cropped haircuts. They were notorious dunkers and high-fliers like their namesake, but they were also quiet and cool and obviously arrogant. They looked at the gym and the spectators and the Badgers most of all with barely concealed distaste. Reggie watched them, his skin prickling.

It was always like this with outside teams . . . like the Badgers were beneath them.

A few of his teammates made remarks or called out challenges. Reggie stayed quiet. He figured it didn't make much sense to talk until they'd proved something—and considering they had lost eight games in a row dating back to last season, they had a *lot* to prove. Rain must have felt the same way, because he was still shooting elbow jumpers, completely oblivious to the Eagles. The others noticed and slowly rejoined the warm-up.

Reggie certainly wasn't proving anything. Grana was taunting him even on game day, and he could still only see the hoop from the dreaded corner three or its evil sidekick, the mid-range two from the wings. And as before, it disappeared only for him, and no one else commented on it. As a result, Reggie had spent most of his warm-up chasing rebounds. He plodded back to the corner now and put up another three—and hit the side of the backboard. His cheeks burned. The gym was filling with spectators, not to mention the visiting team, and he hoped desperately that no one had noticed that horrendous attempt. He could imagine their laughter.

"Please don't do this to me during the game," Reggie said. "Please. Please."

"You talking to yourself again?" Twig asked, jogging by him.

"I don't even know anymore," Reggie muttered.

"Locker room," Rolabi called, already ducking through the door.

It was a normal-size door. He just wasn't a normal-size man.

Reggie followed the others inside, giving the gym a last, whispered *Please*. They filed into the locker room and perched on the benches ringing the walls, staring up at the professor.

"You are afraid," Rolabi said matter-of-factly.

Reggie saw a few players exchange quick looks. He could feel the tension too. Everywhere, legs were bouncing, eyes were wide, hands fidgeting. It was a dangerous place to be a fingernail. He was afraid. Reggie had always "disappeared" on game days, and now the hoop had too. He was wondering if he should feign illness or something. What if he couldn't see the rim on a wide-open layup and he airballed it?

But that too felt outlandish. He had to play ball. This was *game day.*

"Fear is your opponent today, and every day," Rolabi said. "Fear empowers us, but only when we meet it. Today you fear your own assumptions. You assume the arrogant are superior."

"They're really good—" Lab said.

"They are. And if you fear them before we start, then there is no need to play."

Rolabi let the silence hang over the room.

"The fear of others is only a reflection of our own self-doubt," Rolabi continued. "That is a journey you know well. If you bring your weaknesses out there, then you arm your opponent." He started for the door. "Today you face fear. Defeat it, and the score will reflect your victory."

"We can do this," Peño said, jumping to his feet. "Let's shake up the league."

Big John stood up and slapped his chest. "We own this house."

Reggie jumped up too. Adrenaline coursed through him.

"Badgers on three!" Peño said. "One . . . two . . . three . . ."

"Badgers!" Reggie shouted with the rest, throwing his arm up.

He ran out with the team, grinning.

This could be it, he thought, caught up in the excitement. *This could be my day.*

Midway through the third quarter, Reggie hadn't stepped on the court once. In fairness, he could see why. It was a close game, and

Rolabi had trimmed the bench accordingly. Only Big John and Jerome were getting any real minutes from the bench. Vin had played a few possessions, but he had turned over the ball twice to the hard-pressing Eagles, and Peño had gone right back out again, exhausted as he was.

The Eagles were *highly* favored, which was usual for teams outside the bottom. They had been wearing their insufferable smirks right until tip-off. But they weren't smiling now. The Badgers were up by two, and the Eagles were struggling against their well-organized defense—a rapidly shifting zone, which was stifling their high-flying wing players. There were no lobs today. No dunks. There was not much space to work with at all, in fact, and Reggie could see the Eagles players getting frustrated.

He was itching to play, but he knew it wasn't likely. He watched as Rain made another layup on a backdoor cut. As usual, Rain was playing brilliantly. The game seemed to warp and flow around him like ocean currents swirling around a rock. It was still early, but it already felt like the assumed victory was slipping away from the Eagles. Agitated, they attacked again, swinging the ball along the perimeter. But Rain was ready. He had four steals already, and he pounced for a fifth. Or . . . he tried. His opponent charged into him, colliding shoulder to shoulder, and the ref blew his whistle.

"Foul on number seven, West Bottom Badgers."

"What?" Rain shouted.

"Bull—" Peño started.

Rolabi turned to him, and Peño instantly fell silent.

Reggie shook his head. That was Rain's fourth foul, and at least the third questionable call he'd taken—these refs were from another town outside of the Bottom as well, and there seemed to be a very clear bias against the Badgers, and Rain in particular. The bench grumbled.

Barely a minute later, Rain drove into the lane, was hit by another defender, and was called for a charge. The spectators erupted with boos. The Badgers shouted. But Rain was out.

As he stormed over to the bench, still talking to the official, Rolabi called a time-out and gathered the team. Despite their agitation, everyone fell silent as he loomed over them.

"We face many difficult obstacles on the road," Rolabi said quietly. "At times, all we can control is our own reaction. Fortunately, that is the most important detail of all. And each challenge is a chance to build fortitude. We will need it." He turned back to the court. "Rain played well. But if our team has but one wheel, we can only drive in circles. Reggie, you're up."

Reggie swallowed around the lump in his throat. "Yes, sir."

"You got this," Rain said. "Take it home."

"Right," Reggie said weakly. "Thanks."

The team headed back onto the floor, and Reggie fell in behind them. His hands clasped and unclasped at his sides. He tried to breathe. The team needed him. This was his chance to contribute something. He needed to perform. He needed to.

You are so going to blow this, he thought glumly.

Twig patted his shoulder. "Go get it, bro."

The Badgers fell back into a 3-2 zone as the Eagles inbounded the ball and charged up the court.

The opposing shooting guard was a wiry, agile player named Raj, and Reggie knew right away that he was in trouble. Reggie tried to keep a low, open stance, but Raj was lightning quick, and Reggie struggled to stay with him. After firing off a pass, Raj faked left, and Reggie overstepped to block him. Realizing his error, Reggie tried to recover and go right, but his upper body was still swaying left. Raj got the ball again on the cut, dribbled into the paint, and popped the jumper.

Reggie grimaced and ran up the court. His first play, and he'd blown his coverage.

"Three!" Peño called as he dribbled over half-court.

"No Rain, no chance," Raj said. "You about to get smoked, boy."

Reggie flushed. "No we're not."

Nice smack talk, Reggie thought. *You're as quick with that as you are on your feet. Ugh. Focus!*

The third variation was simple: the shooting guard cut to the basket, using a screen from Twig to get open. But while everyone was watching Rain—Reggie, in this case—Lab crossed along the baseline and hopefully got open for the corner three. It was usually an effective play.

Reggie took off into the paint as planned, using the screen. Raj was right on his shoulder as planned . . . but Reggie was *not* Rain. The rest of the Eagles paid him no mind whatsoever, and Lab was guarded tight all the way across. So, Peño threw a bounce pass down to Reggie instead.

"Get a bucket!" Peño shouted.

Reggie turned, trying to take the ball to the hoop and hoping desperately that it would be there. It was—but it was the size of Gran's old wedding band, barely big enough to fit a marble.

"No," Reggie murmured, feeling his heart sink. "Not now."

He realized much too late that he wasn't protecting the ball. Raj stripped it and drove up the court again, and he vaguely heard Lab shouting, "What are you waiting for, Reggie?" Reggie sprinted back, his cheeks blazing, while Raj played a give-and-go and easily laid it in for the tie.

"Take the shot, Reggie!" Peño said.

Reggie felt like he was breathing through cotton. He sprinted up the court again, sparing a quick look at Rolabi—hoping he, at least, might know what grana was doing to Reggie. But the professor just stared back at him, expressionless as always.

Rain was waving him on from the bench. "You got this, Reggie!"

He's right, Reggie thought. *Just relax.*

Reggie tried to calm down. But his lungs didn't listen. They filled and squeezed on their own. His limbs tingled as his blood abandoned them for the bass drum in his chest. Even his eyes seemed to cloud. Everything was moving so fast. The noise was deafening. Shouts and squeaking shoes and calls from his own teammates. He had been in this moment a thousand times in his head. He was here when he was daydreaming at school. He was here when he was shooting rolled-up socks into his trash can. But whenever he got here in a real game, the moment grew beyond him. He was crushed by the weight of it.

He was sure he imagined it, but for a moment, he thought the floor began to tilt inward like a cone, and his shoes seemed to slip along the hardwood. The long fall was waiting for him.

No, he thought firmly. *I can do it. I can do it.*

Even to him, it sounded more like a plea.

Peño went left this time, getting the ball to Lab on the wing. But it really didn't matter where the ball started—the Spotlight Offense meant that everyone had to move. Cash stepped out from the block, and Reggie used him as a screen, cutting toward the open free-throw line. Lab saw him and passed the ball. Reggie caught it, then stopped sharply, letting Raj sprint past.

Reggie now had the ball, and space, and a decision. Should he get the ball to Twig, who was still posting up down low? Take the jump shot? Or drive right to the rim for a strong layup?

Reggie couldn't decide, so he did a bit of each.

He dribbled in a few feet, stopped for a jump shot, and then saw a hand rising up to block him. Stymied, he tried to dump the ball to Twig on the low post. But it was too late. The pass was deflected, stolen, and on its way back up the court before he even had a chance to react. Naturally, Raj got the lead pass and laid it in, giving the Eagles the two-point lead. Reggie felt his guts roiling. He was throwing the game away. He could almost hear his teammates' thoughts:

Typical bench player.

Give the ball up, stupid!

We need Rain!

And another voice, his voice, said: *They're right. Get back to the bench.*

Reggie sprinted up the court, deciding that he would stick to the outside this time and avoid the ball if at all possible. Just a filler. But as Reggie crossed center court, his eyes widened.

"No," he whispered. "Not now."

A slow-creeping fog was leaking out from under the packed

bleachers, right beneath the feet of the oblivious fans. Tendrils snaked their way across the hardwood like grasping fingers, and the fog began to rise up past his knees. He looked to Twig, almost in desperation, but his closest friend was focused on the game. The fog had come for Reggie alone, and the cool dampness settled on his skin, sending goose bumps and tingles racing up the small of his back.

Please not now, he thought desperately.

More and more fog poured in. Soon, white-gray plumes stretched toward the ceiling, obscuring the entire court, and it became hard to distinguish shapes or colors. Reggie squinted, trying to make out Peño. The sound of a ball dribbling seemed to come from all directions, muted and distant. Reggie wanted to scream in frustration.

"Four!" he heard Peño shout through the gloom.

Four, Reggie thought. *Get to the point!*

He was supposed to use a screen from Peño, but Reggie missed him in the fog. He stumbled blindly to the top of the circle, searching for Lab, or Twig, or anything. Condensation beaded along Reggie's arms, joined by salty, nervous sweat. He looked around wildly.

"Hello?" he said.

"Get to the far wing!" someone called.

Reggie spun around, squinting. Did Twig say that? Or Peño?

"Someone support him!"

An Eagles player came cutting out of the mist with the ball and dribbled past Reggie. Instinctively, Reggie chased him, always a step behind, until the player laid it in. The Eagles were now up by six. The mist grew even thicker, like a fading dream. Or a nightmare.

Reggie tried to play through it, but after a few minutes, he decided to avoid the action at all costs. That was easy enough on offense, but less so on D. On that end, his searching hands found only mist, and Raj was past him, laying it up again and again. Numbly, he heard his teammates giving up.

When the final buzzer went off, seemingly hours later, the fog vanished instantly. Reggie doubled over, his hands on his knees, bile rising in his throat. He gagged, trying not to vomit.

"Why is this happening to me?" he whispered.

The Eagles were celebrating nearby: they had won by a comfortable twelve points. His teammates headed for the locker room, scowling, angry, defeated. He almost wished the fog would return to obscure their faces. Rolabi looked at Reggie, who turned away. He'd been unplayable. A complete disaster.

And that, he supposed, was to be expected. But it didn't lessen his humiliation.

When Reggie joined the team in the locker room, he sat alone, ignoring both the annoyed looks from some players and the half-hearted encouragements from Twig. The lights seemed to dim like windswept candles. The drop ceiling sagged on its aluminum crossbeams. Reggie wondered if grana could be broken. Distorted. If it could, he should have known *he* would be the one to do it.

Clearly, it couldn't be controlled. Clearly, Reggie didn't belong on that court.

Rolabi ducked into the locker room, shut the door behind him, and stood silently in the middle of the room. His presence sent a hush over the team. Then he turned directly to Reggie.

"We are only as strong as our weakest link," he said. "That is the lesson today."

This time, Reggie held his gaze. It hurt, but right now, Reggie didn't want any false sympathy. He didn't want a pat on the back. He wanted to feel the sting of the truth.

And Rolabi wasn't done.

"Some people let fear of failure guide them. And in doing so, they fail everyone."

"I don't understand," Peño said.

"The ones who must understand do," Rolabi replied.

With that, he turned and stormed out of the locker room, letting the door slam behind him. Nobody spoke. Nobody looked at Reggie. Rolabi was right: Reggie understood perfectly.

He'd gotten his chance, and he'd blown it.

He doubted he would ever get another one.

SMACK TALK

All people are magnets.
They simply must choose to push or pull.

✧ WIZENARD ⑤⑥ PROVERB ✧

THE NEXT DAY, Reggie stayed in bed late—even for a Saturday. Gran was long gone to work when he finally dragged himself
into the kitchen, ate half a bowl of porridge, and cast himself
down onto the couch with a thud.

P glanced up from her book. "You look awful."

"Thanks."

"Want to play the word game?"

He sighed. "Not right now."

She went back to her book. "You get to dust today."

"Super," he murmured, staring up at the white ceiling stained
with yellow rings of smoke—most of it from his cooking. He
wasn't sure if he was worse at ball or in the kitchen.

"Are you brooding again?"

"Yes."

"Gran says you have coping issues."

Reggie groaned. "What?"

"I asked her why you were so grumpy lately. I thought maybe it was just because of basketball. You know . . . all the losing."

"Yes, I got that, thank you. It's not basketball. Well, maybe. I don't know."

"Maybe you should stop playing."

Reggie sighed. "I can't."

"Why?"

"Because I love the stupid sport. It just doesn't love me back."

P thought about that for a moment. "That's how I feel about asparagus sometimes."

"What?"

"Well, it's delicious, but then you eat it, and your pee smells—"

Reggie stared at her. "It's definitely not the same."

She nodded thoughtfully and started reading again. "Maybe like Gran and yams—"

"It's not like a food," Reggie cut in, sitting up. "It's the one thing in the world I really want to do. No . . . *need* to do. It's the one place I feel happy. And all it ever does is kick me in the butt. It's like deep down I know what I am supposed to be. I know it. And yet every single day I wake up and realize I'm not. I have to look at myself in the mirror and say, 'You're not what you're supposed to be.' I'll be doing that for the rest of my life. And yeah, maybe I can't cope with that."

Reggie realized he had his hands clenched into fists. He looked at them and lay down again. What was wrong with him? It was like a fire was going unchecked in his guts, flaring up.

P shrugged. "So get better."

"And how do I do that, genius?"

"I doubt that lying there feeling sorry for yourself is helping."

Reggie growled and rolled over. "Just read your book."

"Gran says you have a hard time letting go," she said. "Of Mom and Dad."

"What does that have to do with ball?" he replied, facedown on the couch.

"Nothing, I guess. But it probably has something to do with you lying there."

"This is great," he said. "I'm getting counseling from my little sister."

"Well, you can't afford a real therapist."

He laughed. "True enough. Now let me lie here and feel sorry for myself."

"Can't you dust while you do that?" she asked innocently.

Reggie thought about that, and then dragged himself up to find a cloth.

"You're becoming more like Gran by the minute," he muttered.

The next week crawled by. Reggie attended practices, of course, and he was the first to arrive and the last to leave. But he just went through the motions. He took his shots and ran his laps and played his role on defense. He didn't bother with the five hundred makes. He shot from the corner and the mid-range two and missed more than he made.

At school, Reggie was even more distant than usual. He showed up and did his work, and answered questions when he was asked. He smiled when someone told a joke. He exchanged props with his teammates in the hallways. A few times a day, he jolted out of a daze, feeling like a stand-in for himself.

At home, he read the new book that Twig had found. But no matter how many times he scrolled over the text, he couldn't learn anything that seemed important or find any clues about why his mother had given him that box. He held the box at times, but only to think about what he had lost. He took shots with his rolled-up socks, but he knew that his fantasies would never come true. One night, Reggie wondered if that fire in his belly, the *need* for ball, would burn out soon.

He wondered if that would be for the best.

When Friday came again, he went to school, walked home, and set off for the game early as always. It was the Dartmouth Devils tonight—a middle-of-the-road team from about an hour outside the Bottom's perimeter—and Reggie figured the Badgers had a decent chance to win. But this time, he wasn't fool enough to think the chance was his. He just needed to show up, play whatever small part he could, and hope not to embarrass himself too badly. That, it seemed, was the role basketball had given him. He knew now that he couldn't control his grana—he just had to hope it would leave him alone. Reggie suspected he wouldn't be playing today anyway, so it didn't really matter. He tried to console himself with that. It was safer there.

So, when the warm-up was over, he found his spot on the bench, and waited.

Surprisingly, he got a two-minute run in the first quarter, and another three minutes in the second. He managed a defensive rebound and an assist, but he refused to shoot. He fully expected the rim to disappear at any moment, or shrink, or for grana to simply skip all that and drop him in a hole. He kept his head down and tried to keep his temper in check. He felt disengaged from the game, but it was still better than the alternative. He was desperate not to trigger anything. He just wanted to get through the game without any more embarrassments.

They were down three at the half. The Devils were organized and big, but they had no natural scorers like Rain, and they struggled to create. The problem was they were winning every battle in the paint. Pushing guys off rebounds, posting up, hand-checking in the lane. They were physical and persistent and rough. They also liked to talk. A lot.

"How you guys even Elite Ball with one half-decent player?"

"These kids are *weak*. Somebody get this boy a sandwich."

"No good ball team is ever gonna come out of a place called the Bottom."

But the Badgers were used to it. Reggie was used to it. He kept his mouth shut.

Rolabi led the team into the locker room at halftime.

"We are playing well," he said, "but drills and plays mean nothing without constant execution. I can accept missed shots. That is part of the game. But I do not accept surrendered rebounds, lazy shifts on defense, or reluctance to dive for a ball. Those small gains add up to victory."

His eyes went to Reggie, who immediately turned away.

"That means *everyone*. If even one brick is loose, the entire wall will tumble."

He swept out to the gym again, and the team followed, most bouncing on the balls of their feet and clapping one another on the shoulders. Twig fell in beside Reggie, taking a last swig of water.

"Going to be a close one," Twig said. "We're going to need you out there."

Reggie snorted. "I doubt it. Go get us a win. We don't want to go O and three."

"Why don't we both get us a win?" Twig replied, frowning. "Take those shots, man!"

"I just need to work on my defense and—"

Twig stepped in front of him, blocking the door. "You passed up on, like, six open looks."

"I just wanted to keep the ball moving—"

Twig folded his arms. "Play the game. Come on. You worked to be here."

"Yeah," Reggie said, stepping around him. "And I'm here. Let me do my part."

He ignored Twig's protests and walked back into the crowded gym, hearing the cheers and applause as the teams took the floor again. Twig sprinted past him, giving him a last glare.

Reggie planted himself on the bench, annoyed. What did Twig know about Reggie's struggles out there? Twig was a budding star.

Rain was first and foremost on the Badgers, of course, but Twig had really come out firing this year. He was a ball player. He had a chance.

Reggie's eyes flicked to Gran and P in the stands. P glanced at him, and he averted his eyes, strangely ashamed. Why? He had sat on this bench a thousand times. He had long ago accepted who he was. Reggie was destined to sit here, and clap, and watch the game pass him by.

But that thought didn't ring true. It didn't explain why he *had* to be here. It didn't explain why he shot a thousand rolled-up socks into his wastebasket every night. It didn't explain his constant dreams of basketball glory. Anger stirred as the game began. He knew the truth of it.

He hadn't given up on the game. The game had given up on him.

The third quarter raged in front of him. The Devils had obviously expected an easy win, and they were getting frustrated. The Badgers had come out strong to start the half, and Rain was lighting it up from the three-point line. Reggie watched his silky smooth release. He tried not to be jealous, but it was hard. He truly liked Rain. Since training camp, Rain had become a leader to go along with his skills. But in the end, Rain had the gift, and Reggie didn't.

"Just play your role," Reggie whispered.

He was suddenly reminded of his first year on the Badgers. It was two years before Rolabi arrived, and Reggie had been selected to the team over thirty other hopefuls after a long, grueling tryout. It had been a very proud day. Freddy Baines, the coach at the time, had said the new team was going to grow together for years and become real prospects. He said they all had a bright future. Reggie had gone home that night thinking, *It's finally happening*. Gran had even baked him a cake to celebrate. She told him how proud his mom would be.

And then Reggie choked the first game. And the next. And then he was sent to the bench.

"It's all good, bro," Freddy said, "some guys are practice players. Maybe not always, but for now. You always play well in practice. You push Rain to keep working. That's a big job. Everyone has to play their part, Reg."

And so Reggie went to the bench and started showing up early for practices. Not to get ready for games, but to allow himself a few minutes to shine. Alone in the gym—that was the only time he deserved to take shots. Three years later, he was still on the bench, holding on to his spot on the team simply because he was helping Rain.

Reggie felt pressure build behind his eyes and blinked it away, horrified. Crying in front of a packed gym was just what he needed. Why was he even upset? He was in Fairwood Community Center on game day. This was what he wanted. He just wanted to be near the game.

I wanted more, a soft voice said in his head.

The third quarter ended, and Reggie stood at the edge of the huddle, hearing nothing.

But five minutes into the fourth, Rolabi called his name. Reggie looked up, shocked, and then hurried to the scorekeeper's table to wait for a whistle. He tried to fire himself up. He'd been spacing out for an hour, and all the energy had gone out of him. Reggie hopped on his toes.

"Lab!" he called, waving him off, and then hurried onto the court in his place.

Rolabi still believes in you, he thought. *You have to play well. You have to.*

The game started again. Both teams were playing man defense, so he found himself trailing or being trailed by a husky, snub-nosed small forward who seemed to go by "Pipes." That may have been a reference to his abnormally large biceps, which even stacked up against the muscular Cash. Reggie felt like a toothpick next to him, and Pipes clearly saw him as one.

"Post me up," Pipes said on defense, grinning. "Come on. I'll snap you like a wishbone."

Reggie ran around the perimeter, ignoring him. When he got the ball, he swung it back again, or hit Twig on the low post. Two or three times he got open in the corner with the ball, but there was no chance he was taking that shot. He'd seen more than enough air balls in practice. On defense, Reggie fought with Pipes as the stocky forward cut into the paint, swinging his elbows.

"Watch those teeth," Pipes said. "Can't afford no dentist here."

Pipes got the ball in the post and backed up. He stepped onto Reggie's shoe and stuck his butt out at the same time, sending Reggie toppling backward onto his tailbone. Reggie could only watch as Pipes laid it in, smirking.

"Stay down," Pipes said. "Right where you belong."

For a second, he had seen another face looming over him. *Right where you belong.* It had never actually happened, of course, but he had dreamed that scene a million times. President Talin looming over him, smiling cruelly, kicking him back down whenever he tried to stand.

"Let's go, Reggie," Twig said, hoisting him up. "Get him back!"

"Yeah, definitely," Reggie said, trying to shake the image. His blood was boiling now.

The Badgers attacked again. But Pipes was clearly sensing weakness. He jabbed Reggie in the ribs whenever he ran by. He charley-horsed him when the referees weren't looking. Stepped on his toes. The lead changed again and again, the pace quickened, and Pipes methodically wore Reggie down.

"They gonna bench you soon or what?" Pipes said into his ear. "You're weak, bro."

"Can you even shoot the ball?" Pipes mocked. "What you here for? You afraid? Good. You should be."

And after another power layup: "Go home, boy. Save yourself this embarrassment."

Reggie bit his lip, needing to channel his anger and humiliation into something, somewhere, and finding nothing more suitable. He wasn't sure if it was fatigue or grana or what, but he kept seeing Talin's gaunt, skeletal face instead, saying the exact same words.

You're weak. You afraid? You should be.

With four minutes left, Pipes got close on defense again, pushing Reggie out toward the perimeter, dominating him as he had done every minute since Reggie had come into the game. He tried to channel his strength, but his mind was scattered, and his body felt powerless.

"I hope Mommy and Daddy aren't watching today," Pipes said. "They must be ashamed."

Reggie's eyes went to the crowd. To where they might have been sitting. And now he heard *his* voice whispering in his ear. The man who knew exactly why they weren't, and why they never would be.

Something deep and dark stirred, and Reggie turned around, clenched his fists, and punched Pipes hard across the chin. Pipes fell back, stunned, and Reggie followed, shoving him down, getting ready to swing again, but grasping hands pulled him off. Fans were screaming, and through the fog of his anger, Reggie vaguely registered some of his teammates fighting with the Devils.

Rolabi broke it apart, of course. He strode into the fray and separated the teams like they were kittens. Twig was the last to stop fighting. He had someone in a headlock until Rolabi grabbed him by the collar and lifted him off the floor. The referees were in an uproar. The other coach was on the court now too, screaming, pointing at Reggie, demanding that he be ejected.

In the end, three Badgers were ejected: Reggie, Twig, and Big John. Rolabi sent them to wait in the locker room while the game ended, and Reggie sat there in silence, listening to Big John mutter about cornering the Devils in the parking lot. Reggie was too ashamed to look up.

He knew when the others shuffled in that they'd lost. They

plunked onto the benches and waited for Rolabi. The professor said little—only that they had let themselves down. Reggie knew who he meant.

Reggie waited for the team to leave, feeling a few sympathetic taps on his shoulders. Maybe they knew why he had snapped. Or maybe they knew he was in a whole lot of trouble.

"Talk tomorrow, man," Twig said, leaving last of all.

Reggie knew the professor was still in the room. His presence felt like a storm cloud about to burst. But he didn't speak, so Reggie picked up his bag and started for the door.

"I know what he said."

Reggie paused by the door.

"And I know who you saw," Rolabi continued quietly.

Reggie didn't turn back. He just stood there, fighting for control.

"I am sorry your parents are gone. I am sorry that boy said those things to you."

Reggie wiped his nose, nodding, not sure what he was supposed to say.

"But if we cannot channel our emotions productively, they will break us. And as you saw tonight, if even one player loses control of his behavior, he can bring the whole team down with him. I cannot have that, Reggie."

Reggie nodded again, feeling his eyes well up once again. This time, he let them.

"You are suspended for the next game. Take the next two weeks to practice hard. But also take the time to think. And think hard. If there is another incident, you will be off this team."

"Yes, sir," Reggie managed.

He opened the door and went to leave.

"And, Reggie?" the professor said.

Reggie paused in the doorway. "Yes?"

"On my team, each player chooses their role. They are limited only by what they can *earn*."

Reggie nodded, feeling the first tears spill, and hurried out of the gym, eager for the walk home and time to think. But when he stepped into the parking lot, he slumped. Gran was waiting.

And she did not look pleased.

GROUNDING

Your mind is a filter; when it is clouded,
you cannot see the light.

✧ WIZENARD ⑯ PROVERB ✧

REGGIE WAS GROUNDED for two weeks. It was a theme, apparently. He was allowed only to go to school and practice. On the plus side, those were the only two places he ever went anyway.

Perhaps realizing this, Gran added two weeks of bathroom cleaning to go along with the sentence. Since Rolabi had not called a Saturday practice, Reggie had the weekend to sit and mope . . . and scrub the toilet twice a day. Well, that, and ice his very swollen, very sore knuckles.

P took pity on him, at least, and insisted they read together and play a juggling game with her soccer ball when Gran was out. But mostly, Reggie just wanted to be left alone. He felt no pride in starting the fight. He may well have lost the Badgers another game.

Reggie wanted to avoid ball in general—swore to himself he

would—but as always, he found himself draining one rolled-up sock after another, whispering his own narrative, feeling the call of the court every second of the day.

To pass the time, he made some notes from the book . . . details he thought might be important at some point, even if he wasn't exactly sure why:

- Emotional amplitude is the key to broader change

- Fear is the most contagious; the easiest; the most transformative

- A Wizenard is the spark; a Muse is the burning flame

- Grana is in all; but dormant in most; corrupted in some; alight in the few

His notes made little sense, even to him, but he ran his fingers over the symbols and shapes in the illustrations, especially the one that matched his box. He felt drawn to those elegant lines more than ever.

At night, he lay awake and wondered what practice would be like on Monday.

Within ten minutes of Rolabi's entrance, the answer was clear: practice on Monday was *hard*. Backbreaking, sweaty, grind-it-out hard.

Reggie barely had a chance to speak with the others. Rolabi had skipped any sort of opening remarks, his eyes dark gray like the sky at dusk, and simply ordered the team to start running. There was no mention of how long or how far they would go.

Reggie did exchange a few words with Twig, at least.

"Thanks, man," Reggie said, giving him props as soon as he came in.

"Of course. If my best friend gets in a fight with loudmouth idiots, then so do I."

Reggie stared at him, fighting back a smile.

"Did I just say best friends?" Twig said. "I sound like a six-year-old, don't I?"

"Maybe," Reggie replied. "But best friends sounds good. I got your back too."

"Well, try not to punch any more people. I got grounded."

"Me too," Reggie said. "I got to clean toilets every day now. Twice a day."

They broke out laughing then . . . but no one was laughing anymore.

Reggie was actually grateful for the run, though he didn't mention it to the others. He wanted to move on from the humiliation of his fight. No one seemed to blame him—Peño just commented that he had a nice right hook—but he knew he had thrown their rhythm, not to mention getting their second-best player ejected along with him.

Rolabi finally called a halt to the running twenty minutes later, though only for a water break and a quick transition to leapfrogs, wind sprints, and push-ups. They kept at the push-ups until they all face-planted, and Reggie's chest felt like someone was standing on it. He slowly stood.

"We are now O and three," Rolabi said. "We have a twelve-game season. The clock is ticking."

"So is my heart," Big John muttered.

"Today we work on strength. I have brought along something familiar."

Rolabi dug into his bag, pulled out a folded piece of rubber, and cast it out onto the floor. Instantly, it began to inflate, growing taller and taller until the infamous castle formed. This time, it was rounded at the base and two levels higher, with fewer openings in the walls and a raised platform at the top that looked like it had to be *climbed* to reach. It would be very tough to attack.

"I can already feel the bruises coming on," Peño said.

Rolabi dumped the red-and-blue pads and helmets onto the floor. "Begin."

The rest of the week was much the same. They drilled hard, ran harder, and moved through a wide range of familiar magical drills: the castle twice more, each time with a new design; facing off against the tiger, Kallo; and shooting from the mountaintop. Rolabi also introduced some new challenges: tug-of-war with their shadows over a looming precipice; making passes in an archery range where the circular targets ran around on wooden legs; a rebounding drill with teammates' hands fused together; and even a game of dodgeball where they were only allowed to slide like they were on the defense—and with the ball on fire, of course. Reggie did his part through them all. Nothing more. Nothing less.

As game day approached, he longed to play, but he knew Rolabi wouldn't waive his suspension. And as before, the professor was the hardest on him. Reggie knew he deserved it.

When the team broke off at the end of Thursday's practice, Rolabi told Reggie to stay behind for a moment. Reggie perked up and hurried over once the others had left, wondering if he might get a chance to play after all. Even a few minutes might give him a chance to somewhat redeem himself.

"The suspension stands," Rolabi said immediately, quashing that hope. "I do not hand them out lightly, and I do not retract them when I do. Show up in your street clothes tomorrow."

Reggie nodded, trying to hide his disappointment.

"Have you done any thinking?" Rolabi asked.

"Well, yes. I mean . . . what about?"

"What you want from this game. Want you want from your life."

Reggie looked at his feet. "Oh. No. I haven't thought about that."

"I see. What do you think your role on this team is?"

Reggie paused. "Practice hard. Fill in minutes. Try and make them count—"

"I don't want a player who is complacent. I only need players who want more."

Reggie shifted uncomfortably. "I do want more—"

"Do you? I need to see it. And if I don't see it soon, you will be asked to leave the team."

"What?" Reggie breathed.

"I do not punish lack of talent. But I always punish *wasted talent*. See you tomorrow."

He strode from the gym, and the doors slammed behind him like a thunderclap. Reggie felt his knees buckling. Leave the team? This was all he had. Reggie would be lost without ball.

He stared out at the empty court, anger stirring in his belly once again.

"Go ahead and take this too," he shouted at no one and everyone, grabbing his duffel. "Take everything. I'm done."

He stormed out of the gym and walked home, alone as always.

Game day felt strange from the moment Reggie woke up. Usually, game days began with a flutter in his stomach—a sense of anticipation. Today it was a dull, empty ache. He lay in bed and decided that even the faint, usually disappointing chance of a great game was better than *this*.

"Morning," P said, poking her head in. "Ready to watch with me in the bleachers today?"

Reggie groaned and rolled over. "I still get to sit on the bench, P."

"Well," she said huffily, "I didn't want you to sit beside me anyway."

She stormed away, and Reggie sighed into his pillow. He slouched through school. He slouched through dinner—and during both toilet scrubs. He slouched on the bus as he rode to Fairwood in some jeans and a hoodie, forehead pressed against the glass and feeling every bump.

He supposed he didn't need to arrive an hour early, but it was habit now, and he just sat there and watched the others warm up. The Pickering Panthers strutted in, and he felt miserable.

The game didn't improve his mood. It was hard fought, and close, and in the end the West Bottom Badgers lost by seven, and they all shuffled into the locker room and dropped onto the benches. Reggie had been powerless. Detached. His hands had itched for the ball. His feet had burned for the run.

Now Reggie knew exactly what it would be like to not play ball anymore.

It would be awful.

"We can't buy one," Peño muttered, playing with his thumbs.

"O and four," Vin said. "This is as bad as last year."

"It's worse," Big John said. "Because I thought it was going to be better."

Reggie watched Rain sitting quietly on the far side of the locker room, holding a ball.

"We're not good enough," Rain agreed. "But we need to be. Everyone needs to be."

"How?" Jerome said. "We worked hard all week. We even played pretty good—"

Rain stood, dropping the ball. "And pretty good isn't enough. We need *more*."

"I don't have any more," Lab said quietly. "That was it."

Reggie noticed for the first time that Rolabi had come in. He was standing by the door, listening to the conversation. Everyone turned to him expectantly, but he just glanced at Reggie and walked out. Silence fell over the room. The team eventually changed and filed out, until only Twig and Reggie were left.

Twig leaned against the wall, sighing. "I really thought we were going to grana them."

"That's still not a thing," Reggie murmured.

"Well, maybe it should be." He patted Reggie on the shoulder on his way to the door. "You know you're not wearing a uniform, right? You don't actually need to change today."

Reggie stood up and followed him out of the locker room.

"I'm not so sure about that," Reggie murmured to himself.

THE REPORTER

The defeated look at the night sky and see their own insignificance.
The dreamer sees their potential.

❖ WIZENARD ⑥₁ PROVERB ❖

REGGIE WAS ALONE in his bedroom when Gran came in. It was around midnight, and she had a mug between her hands, a tendril of steam rising off it like that Fairwood fog. There was just enough moonlight seeping in for Reggie to see the worry on her face. There seemed to be a lot of that there lately.

Gran clicked on the bedside lamp and sat down, handing Reggie the mug. A sweet yet sharp aroma wafted up, and a memory stirred: his mother sitting by a window, staring out at the sunrise. She used to sit there and drink from a steaming mug every single day before she left for work, even while his father ran around getting ready. That was her—calm, collected, in control.

"Peppermint tea," Gran said. "Drink."

He felt a pang in his stomach. It had always been his mother's favorite.

"Did I wake you?" he asked, taking a sip.

"You were as quiet as a mouse. But I can hear self-pity. One of my many talents." She laid a hand on his arm, staring at him. "And I had a funny feeling you might be awake tonight."

Reggie took another sip, closed his eyes, and breathed in the steam. His eyes nearly watered. If only his mother were here. If only, if only, if only . . .

He shook the thought away. Were there any words that caused him more pain than those two?

"You looked miserable the whole game."

"Yeah," he admitted.

"Why?"

He frowned. "Because I couldn't play."

"You looked miserable the week before. And the week before that too. Why?"

"Well . . . I mean . . . I wasn't playing *well* for those games—"

"So which is it?"

"I don't know. I want to play. I want to play well. I want to be good—"

Gran shrugged. "So do it."

"What, did you and P have a seminar on this?" he grumbled.

"Your father was a good soccer player when he was a boy. Good . . . not great."

Reggie frowned. "What does that have to do with—"

"But it wasn't his passion. He liked to write. Always did. And he liked the news. He used to sit in front of the TV and watch the news every single evening. How many kids do that?"

"I'm still not really getting it—"

"He wanted to be a reporter. Of course, we're from Swain

Street. I didn't have money for college, and we both knew it, and I suppose at some point he might have just stopped trying to get there." She smiled. "But not your father. He studied harder than anyone I've ever seen. In high school, he took every class he could, and asked for more homework, more research, more anything. He was insatiable. And, by the end, he had the best grades in the school. He got to go to college on a scholarship—a boy from *Swain Street*—and he got his journalism degree. Ah, Reggie, you should have seen him the day he graduated. The smile on that boy's face. He was proud, more than anyone else there that day, I think. Because it had been really hard, and he'd earned it."

Reggie pictured his father in his black cap and robe, and he smiled with him.

"He met your mother there. She was more than his match, let me tell you. His life was coming along beautifully. It ended too soon, of course. But for me, remembering him in his cap and gown always gives me joy. He had already earned his dream."

She squeezed his fingers.

"I don't care if you become a professional ball player. You have chosen that path. But I do care that you are happy. That you left nothing behind. *You* told me you love ball more than anything. *You* said you wanted to be a professional. *You* claimed that you would do anything to reach that dream. Have you?"

He thought about her story. About his father working day and night.

"No," he said softly.

"Well," she said. "Then I guess you know what to do."

Gran squeezed his hand and shut the bedroom door, leaving

him with the silence and his steaming peppermint tea. He took a big sip, picturing his mother sitting by the window, and his father standing proudly in his graduation cap. Reggie fell asleep smiling with the empty mug perched against his pillow, giving off the last faint whiffs of peppermint.

The next morning, Reggie woke early. When Gran came out of her room, he already had breakfast going, and the smell of bacon tempted P out of bed as well. It was Saturday, and not technically family breakfast day, but he had wanted to surprise Gran before she left for work.

Of course, he had managed to burn the bacon again. He always seemed to be hitting imagined jumpers when he should have been flipping. He laid the plates out, forcing a smile.

"A little overcooked," he murmured.

P snorted. "It looks like a piece of coal."

"It will do," Gran said. "That said, it's a Saturday, dear. It's seven in the morning. You are aware of this, yes?"

Reggie shrugged. "I wanted an early start today."

"On a Saturday?" P asked, yawning and shoveling down some bacon at the same time.

"Well, it's a good thing," Gran said. "P, you can spend a full day on your homework."

"Homework—" P started.

"Yes," Gran said. "And then you can explain the B you got on your last math test."

Reggie glanced at P, surprised. P had been getting straight As for as long as he could remember, and judging by her scowl, she had been just as surprised. She dug into her potatoes.

"I don't care about math," she said through a mouthful.

"And I don't care about bills, yet they seem to care about me," Gran said.

"What are you talking about, P?" Reggie said. "You were always good at math—"

"And now I'm not," she snapped. "I thought we were talking about you."

Reggie exchanged a look with Gran. P was rarely moody, and never about schoolwork. She had always had an easy time with it. Reggie got good grades, but he had to work for them.

"What's going on?" Reggie asked quietly.

P dug into her food. "I don't need math. It's a waste of time."

"Soccer players should still be well-rounded in all subjects—" Gran started.

"I'm not going to be a soccer player!" P cut in, dropping her fork. "You know that. There's only one girls' team in the Bottom, and they're three years older than me. And they still stink. There are no good soccer players in the Bottom, *including* me. Why do you keep bringing it up?"

"Patricia Lynn Mathers," Gran said. "What has gotten into you?"

"Nothing—"

"Tell me," Gran said softly.

There was a tense moment of silence, and then P started to push her food around.

"It was Hagatha," P muttered.

"Not again," Gran said, rubbing the bridge of her nose. "Her name is *Agatha*."

"You've clearly never met her," P said.

Reggie frowned. "What did Haga . . . she say?"

P chewed on her bacon for a moment. "Well, you know Hagatha. She always has to say something. She was making fun of me because I had my soccer ball out in the cafeteria and—"

"I told you to leave the ball at home," Gran muttered.

"*And* she started going on like 'Where do you think you're going with that ratty old ball tied to your feet, anyway? You think you're going somewhere special? That thing belongs in the trash.' And obviously that's not what I think, but she is just so annoying—"

"What does this have to do with your math test?" Gran asked.

"Oh, well, I shoved Hagatha, got in trouble, and then I was distracted for my test. So, you know, now I hate math. And obviously Hagatha was a given."

Gran dabbed the side of her mouth, expressionless. "So we allow the opinions of others to dictate our interests now?" she asked.

"No," P muttered. "It was dumb to get angry. I already know I'm not going anywhere—"

Reggie's heart ached at the tone of her voice. At the *defeat*.

Gran leaned across the table, pointing a wrinkled finger. "Patricia, you can do anything—"

"I set my mind to?" P finished sharply. "Really? I keep hearing people say that. We can all do anything. So how come nobody does? How come everyone is in the *Bottom*?"

"It's a hard road from here, yes—" Gran said.

"It's impossible."

P pushed her plate away and stormed off to her room. Reggie stared at her empty chair.

"Do you want me to talk to her?" he asked.

"Give her some time. I'll talk to her when I get home. Now eat your breakfast."

Reggie sighed and put his fork down. "The bacon really is terrible."

She laughed. "Yes, it is. Before you become a star, you have got to learn how to focus."

"One thing at a time," Reggie said ruefully.

"If I have to eat one more meal of yours, I won't live to see you become a star anyway."

Reggie started clearing the plates, thinking about Gran's story about his father.

"I'm going to be at Fairwood a lot this week," Reggie said quietly.

Gran was headed for the bathroom, but from the corner of his eye, he caught her smiling.

"Good," she said.

9
DEFENSE FIRST

Talent is a seed. To flourish,
it must be watered with sweat.

✦ WIZENARD ⟨67⟩ PROVERB ✦

REGGIE ARRIVED AT Fairwood under a hot September sun. It was a drowsy Saturday morning as usual in the Bottom, and he had taken the bus today to get as much gym time as possible. He listened as it trundled away behind him, carrying no one nowhere.

He faced the gym for a moment, watching the morning sun bake the pink bricks. The first four games seemed to hang over it. The fog. The fight. P's expression in the bleachers. He was almost reluctant to go in. Why *did* he keep disappointing himself? Why did he subject himself to a game that clearly didn't love him back? He could still just walk away.

Reggie stood alone in front of the old community center, thinking, doubting, but ultimately knowing his path. It was, as ever, through those doors. Pain and hope and risk.

Reggie walked into Fairwood, grinning as he always did when he found the doors unlocked.

He changed into his sneakers and walked to the center of the court with his ball under his arm.

He had been thinking a lot about his grandma's story, and he had started to see grana in a different light. She had questioned if he was giving his all . . . What if grana was questioning him too? What if it was dropping him in holes and forcing hard shots and all the rest to test his resolve? What if grana was encouraging him to *work*? Well, it was time to take up the challenge.

"All right, grana, gym, whoever has been kicking my butt. Do it again. I need your help. I don't know if that means falling down holes or disappearing rims or whatever. But I need help."

He took a deep breath.

"I want to be good. No. *Great*. And I don't know what to do. Please help."

He waited for some sort of reply, but there was none. He sighed and went to work.

Today, Reggie didn't even try a free throw or layup in a vain hope for mercy. He marched right to the corner and set his feet where the hoop dutifully popped into view. Reggie started dribbling, letting his muscles limber up. He tried a few jab steps, faking and then crossing behind his back or through his legs. But after five or six dribbles, Reggie looked up, ready to shoot, and paused. The hoop was gone again.

Confused, Reggie walked over to the mid-range two, where the rim reappeared again. He just shrugged and started dribbling, figuring grana wanted him to miss from there today instead.

But as soon as his fourth dribble hit the floor, the hoop vanished again.

"What . . . now I can't even dribble?" he asked aloud.

He pushed down his frustration and tried to think. If grana really was on his side, what would it be telling him? He thought back to the games he had played this season. In fairness, he *had* lost the ball on the dribble a few times—or just delayed and been swallowed up by the fog.

Was he dribbling too much?

Reggie walked back to the mid-range two, took three dribbles, and put up the shot. To his surprise, he swished it. But before he could congratulate himself, the ball shot out like a meteor toward the nearest corner. Reggie quickly retrieved it, ran back to the corner, and took a three-pointer after just one dribble. He missed long, but as soon as the rebound hit the floor, the ball blasted out again, whizzing through the air and smashing into the locker room door.

"Oh," Reggie said, instantly understanding the setup. "Right."

He retrieved the ball, dribbled twice, and shot it . . . waiting just long enough for the follow-through before rushing to the corner and catching the ball that was now hurtling in that direction. Back and forth he ran, putting up seemingly endless transition jump shots. Sometimes he dribbled once or twice, sometimes not at all, but he never went over three, or the rim would swiftly disappear. His calves began to tighten. In time, they throbbed with every extension. His wrists and fingers ached from the hard rebounds. His eyes itched with sweat. His mouth was so parched that he sucked the moisture from his shirt. A hundred shots went up. Then a thousand.

He began to whisper each ball's fate, and often, he knew as soon as it left his fingers.

"Make . . . Make . . . Miss . . . Miss . . . Miss, come on! . . . Miss . . . Make . . . Make . . . Make . . ."

He took a water break, then went at it again. His whispers became shouts:

"Make! Miss! Miss! Focus! Make! Make!"

Both hoops vanished at 250 makes, and, guessing at the cause, he switched to the other side of the floor. They promptly reappeared, and he went again. The time wore on. The pain intensified. Whenever he hit the ground after a jump shot, his knees buckled, threatening to give.

Finally, perhaps hours later, he rose up into a long corner three, flicking his sore wrist.

"Make," he whispered.

The ball swished through the hoop, and he came down into a crouch, catching himself as sweat poured like an open tap onto the hardwood. He stayed like that, aching, sore, and smiling.

Eventually, Reggie shuffled to the bench and sat down, drinking deeply from his bottle. He realized he was still smiling. His body was raw, his fingers and toes blistered, and yet, he felt *relieved*. He had made his five hundred shots from his weak spots. That meant, of course, that he could make them again. He began to pack up his bag . . . and then his shadow rose out of the floor.

"I was thinking about heading home—" Reggie started.

His shadow shook its head, pointing to the court.

"Right," Reggie said. "Never mind."

He walked out onto the floor, preparing to get into attacking position. But his shadow shook its head again and gestured for Reggie to pass it the ball. Reggie hesitated. They had drilled with their shadows before, but never as the *defenders*. His shadow gestured sharply again.

"Fine," Reggie said, tossing the ball over. "Can you even—"

Before he could finish the sentence, his shadow was past him, laying the ball in.

"Dribble," Reggie murmured. "Okay. Fine. Again."

His shadow dribbled back to the top of the circle with a casual ease that Reggie had only ever managed alone. He crouched, getting low and flat and sticking his arms to either side of him like a posturing beach crab. His shadow attacked, and Reggie tried to follow, jerking to a halt. He looked down and saw that his left sneaker was now snuck to the hardwood. The floorboards seemed to have melted into a woody brown glue, and they were steadily pulling him in. Straining, he yanked his foot free, but by the time he did, his shadow had long since scored.

Reggie looked down, checking under his shoe. "What's this about?"

His shadow just dribbled back to the top of the three-point line.

"You know, I might just bring a flashlight next time," Reggie muttered.

He got low again, testing his footing. As before, his shoes were sticking to the floorboards. Reggie was forced to prop himself up on the balls of his feet, his toes primed, trying to keep as little surface area on the maple slats as he possibly could. He found there was a little less stickiness that way, and he was able to slide on his toes, thereby keeping in front of his shadow—which was moving back and forth, as if testing Reggie's maneuverability. Then it attacked.

His shadow drove hard to the left. Reggie managed to slide with it this time, staying well up on his toes. But this time, it was a fake. His shadow cut right instead, forcing Reggie to try to slide back to follow. He managed to successfully adjust his feet—but as usual, his upper body didn't readjust in time. His torso kept swaying left with his momentum, and his shadow drove down the lane and scored a third uncontested layup.

Reggie scowled and waited for his shadow to get back in position again.

"On your toes," Reggie murmured. "Try not to overreact. And . . . ah!"

He yelped as something large plopped onto his head. Reggie reached up frantically, felt feathers, and then promptly received a sharp nip on his fingers. A narrow, beaked face appeared, staring at him upside down with gold-flecked purple eyes. Reggie gaped back at it, unable to move. He had seen them only in pictures, of course, but there was no mistaking it: an emerald-green parrot was sitting on top of his head, and it looked oddly . . . amused. The boy and the bird stared at each other for another moment, until finally, Reggie summoned his courage and took a breath.

"Umm . . . are you a speaking parrot?" he asked.

The parrot blinked, and then proceeded to squawk directly into his face and sit upright again, out of sight but still clamped on his head. Reggie's shadow began to dribble, ready to attack.

His shadow went left, and Reggie instinctively went with it, getting low. Once again, his body swayed on the cut, tipping the parrot. Immediately it dug its claws into his head.

"Ow!" Reggie cried. "Okay . . . get off!"

He tried to wrestle the parrot off, but it hooked its claws even deeper into his scalp, forming the world's worst crown. For added fun, the parrot squawked into his ear, and then chortled, as if entertained. Reggie was definitely reminded of Kallo.

He scowled. "Okay. So I have sticky cement for floor and a bird on my head, and I have to defend my shadow, who for some reason is much better at basketball than I am. No problem."

His shadow dribbled to the top of the circle again. Reggie sighed, positioned himself into a defensive stance—propped on the balls of his feet—and tried to keep his body and neck as straight as possible so as not to disturb the parrot. Mercifully, the bird settled in using slightly less claw.

"Well, parrot, shadow, increasingly ridiculous grana," he said resignedly. "Let's do it."

He was scored on. *A lot.* The first twenty possessions, at least. He was so focused on his footwork and upper body position that he made bad reads and slow shifts. But slowly, inexorably, he stopped thinking about his positioning. His feet remained primed. His back straight. He focused on the movements of his shadow's solar plexus, which didn't seem to lie as well as the ball.

And, in time, he began to make stops.

In response, his shadow backed him into the post, and they wrestled for position down low. Reggie took elbows and shoulders and the stab of claws whenever he lost his balance. They fought until he wasn't even sure if it was Saturday anymore, and then, finally, his shadow handed him the ball, nodded once, and vanished. The parrot took off in a flurry toward the ceiling, where it passed right through the rafters and into a momentary flash of bright blue-green sky. Reggie lay down right there on the floor. He was so tired, he couldn't do anything else. His body felt like overstretched putty; his head like a pincushion.

"Well," he muttered, tepidly climbing to his feet. "I'll see you tomorrow."

10

LIGHT THE FIRE

*Train your mind in conjunction with
your body, or both will fail.*
◆ WIZENARD ⑤⑦ PROVERB ◆

LATER THAT NIGHT, Reggie sat alone in his room with the book again, running his fingers across the symbols on every silken page. He had read the entire book by now, chapters like "Resonance of Surety," "Energy in Biological Design," "Concentric Envy," and more, all with equally odd titles. None of them made any more sense than the first chapter he'd read. Certainly none of them explained how grana worked, and more importantly, how he could get it to work for him.

He glanced at the box. What did that symbol have to do with his parents?

"Would a *slightly* longer note have been too much to ask, Mom?" he said, sighing.

He had debated asking Rolabi, but the professor seemed a little . . . frosty lately, especially toward Reggie. Somehow, despite Rolabi's full, if negative, attention, grana's taunting, and his ever-growing assortment of training creatures, Reggie felt more and more alone. More . . . isolated.

He picked up the box, running his hands over the wood grain. His mother had wanted him to have it. He had thought it was simply to hide the note, but why was that symbol carved into the wood? There had to be a reason. Did she want him to store something inside? He didn't have anything valuable enough to belong in that elaborate box.

He put the book in a drawer and the box back on its usual perch. If only he could *ask* them. Without thinking, he looked toward the door, as if his parents were sitting outside it in the living room, talking, watching TV. He moved toward the door, and then caught himself, and felt his stomach go hard, his limbs heavy. The memories came and went in waves, and he just turned back to his bed, willing them away. They were gone, and the box was empty, and Reggie had to make do alone.

Or did he? He'd asked Gran about the box and the hidden note before, but she had always been stalwart that she didn't know anything and that the note could have been about anyone . . . not necessarily Talin. Reggie was sure she wasn't telling him everything, but she insisted. He did have the book now and the matching symbol, so he supposed it was worth a try.

He scooped up the book and went out to find Gran tidying up some last dishes before bed.

"Look familiar?"

He laid the open chapter out on the table. Gran eyed him for a moment, and then picked up the book, leafing through the pages.

"Where did you get this?"

"Library. Gran, it's the symbol on that box."

She put the book down and returned to her tidying. "Coincidence."

"Are you sure Mom and Dad didn't say anything about it?"

Gran kept her eyes on the dishes. "I don't believe so."

"Gran . . ."

She dried her hands off and turned to him. "I've seen this symbol before . . . even before I saw the box. But I had no idea what it was either. I didn't know about the note, and I still caution you not to read too much into it. It might have been hidden in that old box for a hundred years before you found it."

Reggie tucked the book under his arm. "I'm going to figure it out, Gran."

"There's nothing to figure out."

He scowled and went back to his room, looked through his book again, and waited until Gran had gone off to sleep. He was angry she was holding back, but he was angrier at Talin. This was his fault, Reggie was sure. His parents had published stories about how terrible Talin and his government were, and he had had them killed. It was the only explanation of the crash that made sense. His parents were too smart to just die in some *accident*. That wasn't possible.

Hatred roiled and flopped like a fish in Reggie's belly.

He checked the alarm clock. It was late—well after midnight. That meant that Gran and P were fast asleep. Reggie hesitated, then slipped out of bed.

He did it once or twice a month, and only at night. He threw on a coat, eased out of the apartment, and ran the five blocks to Finney and Loyalist. Or more accurately, to the statue that dominated the intersection. Reggie stopped in front of it, sparing a quick look around. There had been lights ringing the pedestal once, but they had long since burned out. Now the huge bronze statue of the president looked over the city in darkness, lit only by a last few streetlights nearby.

Reggie was alone. That was for the best.

He scooped up a rock, cocked it, and rang it off the statue's big forehead. He did it again and again, and only when he heard voices did Reggie take off running through the night, not stopping until he was bathed in sweat.

Reggie doubled over, hands on his knees, and then walked back to the apartment.

He didn't feel any better. But it was something. Sometimes, he needed *something*.

He spent six more hours training on Sunday. The shadow, the tar-like floorboards, and the parrot all returned, along with a new addition: a giant sandbag slung over his shoulders to keep him low in his defensive stance. Despite it all, he managed to force more and more stops, and he hit his five hundred shots. He also had a calf cramp, a rolled ankle, and three jammed fingers, and he grimaced when he finally lay in bed that night, feeling all the aches and pains at once like he had been lowered into a steel vise. When he slept, he slept like the dead.

The next day, Reggie went back to Fairwood before school.

He had to wake up at five in the morning to do it, but he got in a solid hour of training, then jogged all the way home to shower and get ready to leave again. When he stepped out of the bathroom, P was standing there, shaking her head.

"You're crazy," she said.

"Probably."

She walked past him. "You going to win Friday with all this extra practice?"

He hesitated. "It would be nice."

"We'll see. Try not to get suspended!" she said brightly.

"Thanks for the vote of confidence," he muttered.

That night, he arrived *two* hours early to practice. By the time the rest of the team arrived, he had already completed a full workout on his own and gotten his five hundred baskets. He was exhausted, but he was ready to play again. A mindless, desperate need to improve drove him.

Twig came over to give him props, then stopped, eyeing him.

"How long you been here?" he asked suspiciously.

Reggie shrugged. "A little while. Why?"

"Because you stink," Twig said, and they both burst into laughter.

"Maybe more than a little while," Reggie admitted.

Twig seemed to consider that. "Was it my pep talk?"

"Yours was one of many," Reggie muttered.

Twig grinned. "But mine was the best. I know. Don't say it. I'm just so inspirational—"

He was cut off as a ball smacked into the back of his head.

"Sorry!" A-Wall called.

Reggie patted his friend's arm and went back to his warm-up. "Deeply inspirational."

Rain fell in beside him, pivoting into a turnaround jumper. "Ready for Friday?"

"Yeah. Got to make up for the last few weeks. I won't mess this one up."

Rain left his rebound and turned to him. "You're pretty hard on yourself, huh?"

"What?"

"You're a good player, man," Rain said. "You have all the tools."

Reggie snorted. "If I do, then I definitely don't know how to use them."

"Or won't," Rain said.

Reggie looked at him, forced a smile, and went back to his warm-up. *Won't?* Was Rain implying that Reggie *chose* to be bad? That was ridiculous. Of course Reggie wanted to be good. He wanted to be a great ball player more than anything. This had nothing to do with choice.

Nothing in his life had been chosen. The world chose, and he got to react.

Rolabi arrived fifteen minutes later and called the Badgers to center court.

"This week we have the Trenton Titans," Rolabi said. He fixed his gaze on Reggie first, then the rest of the team. "They are well organized, long, and efficient on the offensive end. It will be difficult."

There was a stir across the team. Reggie knew all about the Trenton Titans. They had placed third in the conference last year and made nationals. The Badgers had an atrocious schedule: the Titans this week, and last year's conference champions the week after. It wasn't a coincidence. All the good teams liked to schedule Bottom games. It was usually an easy win.

"The Titans made the national tournament," Twig whispered.

"This will be our biggest test thus far," Rolabi said. "Win this, and we send a message."

"What message?" Peño asked.

"That the Bottom is back," Rolabi replied simply. "Individual talent will not get us through this game. The Titans are big and physical. We will need to match their physicality with fight and effort."

"From *everyone* this time," Peño said, looking around at the team.

"Here we go," Vin muttered.

"What's that supposed to mean?" Jerome asked.

Reggie knew a few of the guys had exchanged words on the way out of the game Friday. Sitting in his street clothes as a spectator, he'd had the time to focus on those little exchanges. He had figured it was normal frustration, but there had been some definite tension in the air since.

Peño shrugged. "Some guys just aren't fighting out there."

Big John laughed derisively, waving him away.

"Like who?" Vin asked Peño. "Everyone but you?"

"I've been fighting," A-Wall said hotly.

Lab held his hands up. "Just relax, guys—"

"No," Vin said. "He was talking like this last week too. What you saying, Peño?"

Reggie felt a tingle on the back of his neck, like the drape of a feather. He shifted uneasily. The air suddenly seemed warm. Humid. He caught the whiff of wet sock. It was as if Fairwood was reverting to its former self. He frowned. Was the team doing this? He looked at the far wall, where the fresh white paint was beginning to flake away.

Twig glanced at him. "You all right?"

"Yeah. Fine. Do you smell anything?"

Twig sniffed. "No."

"I'm just saying we need to be dogs out there," Peño cut in loudly. "We need hustle."

"I thought we were badgers," A-Wall muttered.

Vin was shaking his head. "Starters always blaming the bench. Typical."

"Today we scrimmage," Rolabi cut in, eyeing the team. "Starters versus bench."

That was unusual—Rolabi hadn't started a practice with a scrimmage since the first days of training camp. Rain nodded at him and began to jump on his toes, clearly getting pumped up. Reggie felt a nervous flutter. When Rain got going, he was tough to stop.

"Begin," Rolabi said. "First to twenty. The losing team runs fifty laps."

"Fifty laps?" Big John said. "Bench team . . . we are not losing to these starting punks."

Lab snorted. "The starters don't lose to the bench, bro. That's why we're starters."

"You lost us the last two games," Vin pointed out, taking a noticeable step toward him.

Reggie looked around. Now there was more than tension in the air. It felt like open hostility. All around him, the paint continued to peel, the rafters creaked, and the heat began to steadily rise. But no one else seemed to notice. He chewed his lip nervously . . . this could get bad.

"Maybe a bit more support would help," Peño replied. "Give us a few breaks."

"Maybe you need a long break," Vin said. "Like a full game on the bench."

The whole gym seemed charged now. Reggie noticed that even Twig had his eyes narrowed. In fact, everyone seemed to be glaring at one another. He supposed an 0-4 start had begun to affect the team. Maybe they had all been waiting for the same magical beginning to the season that he had. Disappointment was sliding into anger.

They split into their respective teams, and the bench players fell back into man defense as the starters advanced. Reggie tracked Rain to the perimeter and was surprised when Rain immediately went to the post instead. Rain got low, anchoring himself and then slowly driving Reggie back toward the hoop. Reggie was knocked off balance, and by the time he found his footing, Rain was firmly on the block, and Peño hit him with a quick pass for the layup.

Reggie scowled and ran up the floor. He wasn't sure why everyone was in such a foul mood today, but he felt it seeping into him as well. The frustration of the last two games. The suspension and the missed opportunities. The realization that nothing at all had changed for him.

This season was supposed to have been different.

Reggie should have known. Nothing came easy in the Bottom.

"Strength on the court comes from our positioning," Rolabi instructed from the sidelines. "We stay low. We gather power from our legs and core and transfer it into our point of impact, wherever that may be. Shoulders, arms, hips. On offense, we use this collective power to carve out our space to operate. On defense, we use it to make our opponents work to earn their own. Reggie was defeated because he was not ready. If we are not ready, then we are preyed upon."

Reggie grated his teeth. It was always *him*. Why did Rolabi have to go after him?

"Run a three!" Vin called.

Reggie tried to get to his spot—he was supposed to set a screen at the point for Vin—but Rain was on him in a second. He bumped and tugged and fought with him the whole way, throwing the timing off and allowing Peño to easily stay with Vin on the cut. Jerome swung the ball back to Reggie at the point, and Reggie held it safely back, surveying the floor.

Everyone was fighting with their check. Big John and Twig were nearly wrestling. Lab and Jerome were hand-checking each other so hard, it looked like a fistfight. Reggie's eyes went to A-Wall, who had cleared some rare space on the block against Cash and had his hand up for the ball. But as Reggie prepared to lob it down to him, Rain closed in, slapping the ball free.

Rain picked it up and sprinted down the court for the easy layup.

"These turnovers, man!" Vin called, glaring at Reggie. "They're killing us."

"How many you have last game, Vin?" Jerome said. "Five in four minutes?"

Vin scowled. "Let's just get a bucket."

The bench players attacked again. This time, they got the ball to Big John on the block, who took a step back, swinging his hips at the same time. He connected with Twig's stomach and sent him sprawling onto the floor. Then he turned and laid it in, staring down at Twig with a cocky grin.

"You better step it up, Stick Boy," Big John said.

Peño raced over and shoved Big John back. "Step away."

"What you gonna do?" Big John asked, bumping his chest into Peño's face.

Reggie glanced at the sidelines, expecting Rolabi to step in, but the enormous professor sat still, his expression unreadable.

Big John and Peño eventually broke apart, and the scrimmage began again. Rain was playing hard on defense . . . bordering on dirty. Reggie felt his temperature rising with each uncalled foul, but he kept quiet and tried to play through it, avoiding the smack talk and confrontations and hostility. He didn't play that game. He didn't like challenging people or getting heated. Over time, though, the physicality began to wear him down. Players were wrestling on the post, talking trash, and fighting hard for every loose ball.

At 15–14 for the starters, Reggie came off a screen and found himself in open space. Eyes up, he drove for the hoop and leapt for the finger roll at the rim. He didn't make it. Rain chased him from behind, and Cash came flying over at the same time for the block. Stranded in midair, Reggie slammed off of Cash's barrel chest and hit the ground, rattling his teeth.

He lay there for a moment, winded, furious.

Reggie was tired of being pushed around. No one had called a foul, and the ball had gone out off Reggie, so he backed up on defense, watching as the starters fanned out in attack. When Rain got the ball, he closed in hard, not giving an inch. Rain tried to back him up, but this time Reggie got low, straining his legs and putting everything into the point of contact on his puffed chest. Rolabi had said he needed to channel his emotions after the fight—and now he understood. He let it pour into his defensive stance, into his ready muscles, and into the single-minded determination to stop Rain.

"Not this time," Reggie growled.

Rain swung the ball away again and rotated to the far side. Reggie followed, but when Peño drove to the hoop, Reggie leaked off and swatted the ball away.

He grinned wolfishly as it flew into the bleachers. His heart was beating madly.

"Boom!" A-Wall shouted. "How's that for the bench?"

When they ran down the floor, Reggie called for the pass on the wing. He backed Rain up, grinding for every inch, and then spun around and laid in a hook shot. He slapped his chest.

"Let's go!" Reggie said.

As he ran back on defense, he realized he had never acted like this before. But today, in this heated gym, he didn't just want to play basketball. He wanted to win. He wanted to *beat them.*

The two teams launched into battle. Every point was contended. At 19–19, Lab missed a jumper from the corner, and Reggie dove onto the floor to recover the long rebound. He rolled away from Rain and tossed it to Jerome on the break, who laid in the transition bucket for the win. Big John grabbed Reggie's arm and hauled him back up again.

"Beast," he said, patting Reggie's chest. "Who woke this man up?"

"Game," Rolabi said. "Starters, fifty laps. I will see you all tomorrow."

Reggie stood still, feeling the heat coursing through his body. He let the competitive fire recede with slow, even breaths.

As the starters ran their fifty laps, Reggie changed his shoes alone at the end of the bench, thinking about Rain's challenge to him. Gran had questioned his commitment. Rain had questioned his pride. They wanted the best from him. Or *for* him, in Gran's case. But could he live up to it? He'd had many good practices in his life, even great ones. But when the game started, and the lights got bright, he faded. What was different now? How could he change that?

Twig plopped down beside him, drenched in sweat. The starters were finished and all getting changed as well. "Did you hear any of that?"

"Any of what?" Reggie murmured.

"Didn't think so . . . you looked a bit preoccupied. Probably not the best time to ask everyone, really. You know, with the tension. Mom says I have an issue with social timing—"

"What are you talking about?" Reggie asked.

"Oh, right. Well, my dad wants me to have the team over on Saturday. Pool party and barbecue and stuff. Can you come? I know it's a decent drive but—"

Reggie frowned. "Your *dad* wants us over? To the north end?"

There was an unwritten rule that people from the West Bottom weren't welcome in the north end.

"Of course," Twig said. "My dad loves ball. And he's . . . happy I'm fitting in."

Reggie caught a bit of hesitation in Twig's voice, but he decided to leave it for now.

"Of course," Reggie said. "I think I can get a few bus transfers. What time?"

Twig looked relieved. "Thanks, man. I'm a little nervous about the others. Big John will probably try and drown me, and my dad can be a bit . . . annoying. Come by any time after twelve."

Reggie gave him props. "After we win on Friday night, of course."

"Of course."

Twig hurried out to catch his ride. Some of the guys were making plans for Twig's pool party. Reggie listened to them as he took a breather, smiling. It would be a first for everyone.

"Can you imagine me on the north side?" Big John was saying. "The Twig family don't know what's coming. I never even seen a pool. You think they got some water wings for me?"

"I really hope so," Peño said, laughing. "And they ain't the Twig family, bro."

"Sure they are." Big John made a formal bow, sweeping his arm in front of him like in the old movies. "Mr. Twig, I'm Big John. Oh, is that Mrs. Twig back there? Charmed, madam."

Reggie just laughed and waited until everyone had left. Then he went back to work.

As he had hoped, his shadow appeared, and they worked on low-post and one-on-ones. Reggie practiced the fakes and fade-aways he'd picked up from Rain, and then fought to defend his shadow on the same plays. When he got beat on a lateral fake, the parrot appeared on his head. When he was slow to shift, the hardwood-tar gripped his sneakers even harder. Cramps squeezed his ribs. His thumbnail cracked and fissured under a hard rebound. His feet went numb.

He worked until even his shadow tired, and then he went to leave. But when he tried to push the front doors open, he bounced right off them. Reggie pushed again, a little harder this time. They didn't budge. He put his shoulder into it. He even tried a kick. Nothing.

The doors were locked.

"Hello?" he called. "Rolabi?"

There was no answer. Reggie charged the doors like a human battering ram. He bounced off and landed flat on his back, forcing the air out of his lungs.

Reggie lay there for a minute or two, staring up at the rafters and reflecting on just how many times he had been lying on the hardwood lately.

"Fine," he said. "You want more work? No problem. I can do this all night."

Scowling, he got up and put his sneakers back on, launching into an easy shootaround—still solely from the corners and mid-range twos. He already had his five hundred makes, so he decided to aim for a thousand instead. He had made another two hundred when he noticed the gym clock hadn't even budged. He wondered if it was broken again. He had no idea how late it was, but he supposed it didn't really matter. He was stuck, so he might as well keep shooting.

After what had to have been another hour or two, Reggie tried the door, found it locked, and went back to shoot more. After making a thousand shots for the day, he sat down on the court for a while, throwing the ball up and down. After what must have been four hours—it actually could have been ten, for all he knew—he started measuring exact distances to the hoop from various spots on the floor. How many steps it took to the hoop from the elbow, or how much room he needed to spin left in the post or fade away into a jump shot inside of the paint.

He recited the numbers like a mad scientist as he walked around:

"Thirteen feet to the hoop, one and a half steps right, one left . . ."

He tried the door once again, growing more agitated.

"Hello!" he shouted. "Anyone? Rolabi? Do we have a janitor? Fairwood ghosts? Hello?"

But his calls went unanswered, his blood boiled, and he went back to work.

When the hours had become seemingly endless, he announced plays for himself and fired the ball off every inch of the backboard from different angles, watching where it went at first and then eventually predicting before he even released it. In time, he guessed right almost every single shot. He did the same exercise off the rim, until he predicted those bounces too. As he grabbed one rebound, the lights flicked off, plunging him into darkness.

"Really?" he said.

He blindly found his way to the door and tried it again. Still locked.

"How is this helping?" he shouted. "I said help me! Not trap me!"

He stood there for a moment, fuming, and then decided to go try to shoot again, jumping up to find the backboard and working outward from there. He remembered a similar drill from training camp, but it was much different alone. The only sounds were his own breathing and the thud of the ball. Reggie couldn't let it stop bouncing on a rebound—he would never find it in the pitch-blackness—so he had to quickly track every rebound immediately. He was like a subterranean hunter launching an ambush. It seemed like days went by in the darkness. The air felt heavy somehow, like molasses, and his muscles grew sore from the constant wary state of readiness. It all wore away at him, and every so often, he lost his patience.

"I got this!" he screamed at the darkness. "I won't quit. I told you I'd earn it!"

He had no idea how long it had been, but eventually, the doors eased open, letting fiery evening sunlight pour inside. The clock sprang back to life, but it ticked only a minute ahead. No time had passed at all. Reggie stared at the open doorway. He could leave now. It was done.

"I want another chance," Reggie said quietly. "I want to earn it."

He turned back to the hoop and kept shooting until the last light faded. He practiced just as hard all week. And when Reggie woke up on Friday morning, he knew he had done everything he possibly could to prepare himself. It was game day, and this time, he was ready.

PINE

The world is not always ready when you are.
It rewards only those who stay ready.

◆ WIZENARD ⬤52 PROVERB ◆

REGGIE WALKED INTO the gym two hours before tip-off. He had already been there before school that morning. He had been there all day, even when he was sitting at his desk, daydreaming in class. Reggie had worked harder than ever this week. He had out-worked the rest of the team. He had outworked his own expectations of himself. He felt he had earned his chance to redeem himself.

Reggie spent the two extra hours shooting, along with warm-ups, stretching, and visualization—something they had worked on with Rolabi throughout the summer. He knocked down the rest of his five hundred makes from the corner and mid-range, and then hit some more. When the rest of the team arrived, he joined the team warm-up and worked so hard that he was dripping sweat in the layup line. His uniform clung to his skin like a banana peel.

And when the Trenton Titans strutted inside, he copied Rain and just kept shooting.

"This is my day," Reggie whispered to himself. "This is my time."

He barely heard the crowd filing in. It was background noise. The only sounds that mattered were the heartbeat of the ball on the floor and the breeze of a perfect swish. He walked to the locker room when it was time and took his seat on a bench and felt his knees bouncing beneath him.

"We need this one," Rain said.

"Bad," Twig agreed.

Lab was tossing a ball between his hands. "They're good, man."

"So be better," Rain countered, looking around the room. "We aren't losing again."

Rolabi ducked into the locker room, then straightened until his short salt-and-pepper hair was brushing the ceiling.

"You all know the situation today. We are O and four this season, and we are about to face improved competition. The type of team that we must defeat if we are to reach our own aspirations. This is a test of your commitment."

"I'm ready—" Peño started.

"Words don't matter," Rolabi cut in. "Show me on the court. If you face your fears and play despite them, if you fight for every possession, and if you want it, if you *really* want this, then we have a chance to change an old narrative." He turned to the door. "Let's see if you do."

They threw their hands up with a cry of "Badgers!" and followed him out to the cheers of their home crowd. Reggie sat on the bench, situating himself right next to Rolabi. He fought the urge to chew his nails as the starters took their spots around Twig at center court and the Titans came out to meet them.

Their chalk-white uniforms and matching shoes gave them the impression of being carved from ice and snow, and they were notoriously coolheaded to match. They were less boastful and brash than the Eagles, and relied on strength, organization, and an obvious self-belief. To Reggie, it was more intimidating than the high-flying Eagles or loudmouthed Devils—these boys had come to do their job and go home. Now it was up to the Badgers to disappoint them.

The game roared into action, and it didn't take long to see why the Titans had gone to nationals last year. They won the tip and moved into a well-rehearsed offensive scheme, swinging the ball around with methodical purpose until Cash switched a touch slow to the corner. The opposing guard slashed right past him to the hoop for an easy, wide-open layup.

Luckily, it also didn't take long to see that the Badgers weren't going to roll over.

They charged back up the court, and Rain drove into the lane, faked the shot, and dished it to Twig for a wide-open bucket. It went back and forth for a few possessions in rapid transition, and then the game finally tightened, and the defense began to grind on both sides. The Titans didn't panic, and neither did the Badgers. Today was going to be a battle of discipline.

Reggie watched as the first quarter went by, barely able to restrain himself from leaping into the play. The Badgers had taken the week's hard practice and brought the same energy: they were fighting on both ends, staying low and channeling their strength into the point of contact. Everyone boxed out on defense. They fought through screens. Stood their ground when they set them. But despite the rigor, only two subs went in during the first quarter: Vin and Jerome. Reggie chewed his nails all the way through. Big John got a run six minutes into the second, fighting hard down low and almost certainly earning himself more minutes for next half.

The game raged on.

At halftime, Reggie tried to catch Rolabi's eyes in the locker room. To shout that he was ready. But Reggie knew that wasn't his place. The professor would call his name, or he wouldn't.

Rolabi said only one word at the half: *"More."*

The teams went at it again. Hard play grew harder, and the discipline began to slip. Rain took a stray elbow in the chin. Cash ran into a Titan and sent him flying out-of-bounds. Even Twig got into a shoving matching down low, and both players got a technical. The Titans coach was a grim man, and he and Rolabi watched stonily from the sidelines, subbing out transgressors.

After every whistle, Reggie turned to the professor, eager for a chance. But Rolabi ignored him. A-Wall got solid minutes in the third along with the others. Every player on the bench had gotten onto the court now and earned their rotation spot. Everyone except Reggie.

"Next change," Reggie muttered to himself as the third came to a close.

"Soon," he said halfway through the fourth.

"*Please,*" he whispered with three minutes on the clock.

Peño drove up the court with two minutes left. The Badgers were down four now, and he was pushing the pace again, fighting around a full-court press. The opposing point guard was tracking him, but he was too close, and Peño was almost impossible to mark in the open floor. As expected, Peño crossed him, creating space and driving to the right. And then he stepped on the defender's foot. Peño's right ankle rolled sharply, and he let out a horrible, gargled shriek.

Peño hit the ground and curled up, grabbing at his ankle.

Rolabi swept out onto the court. Peño's dad leapt up in the stands. Lab rushed to his side. Reggie knew this wasn't a pull or a sprain. He could hear the pain in Peño's voice as he gasped and clutched at his ankle.

Reggie's suspicions were soon confirmed. Rolabi scooped him up and gingerly laid him on the floor next to the bench, gesturing for Peño's father and withdrawing a pack of ice from his medicine bag. After a quick word, Peño's father crouched down next to his older son, patting his shoulder.

"Broken ankle," Rolabi said, turning back to the team. "Vin . . . finish strong."

Reggie felt a pang of sympathy. Broken ankle. Peño would be out for weeks. *Months.*

"I can stay with him—" Lab started, crouching next to his brother.

"Take it home," Peño managed, waving his brother away. "I'm fine. We'll go to the hospital after the game . . . there's two minutes left. Go! I told you . . . I'm way tougher than you."

"Not with all that screaming," Lab said.

"They were battle cries," Peño replied, wincing through the pain. "Go!"

The team re-formed and went back out, with Rain leading a cheer to win for Peño. They tried hard. It was a great ending. A big Twig hook shot with two minutes left. A fadeaway three from Rain. And when it was over, they had lost by seven points, and the Titans were celebrating, and Reggie sat on the bench, stunned. He hadn't stepped foot on the court. Not for a single play.

All of that work, and he had been benched completely.

Reggie was silent through the postgame talk. He was silent as Peño and Lab shuffled out with their father, and as the others left, heads down. Everyone must have known that the season was all but lost. Reggie was silent on the ride home, knowing that *his* season, and his dreams, almost certainly were.

He had worked so hard. Mornings and late nights and every practice. And for all that, he had watched his team lose again from the bench. When Reggie got home, he went right to bed.

Gran and P let him go.

P slipped into Reggie's room a few hours later in her pj's. Reggie could hear Gran snoring from the other room.

He had been awake, of course, staring at the stucco and making shapes in the dim light. She climbed up onto the foot of his bed and followed his gaze, playing with a strand of her hair.

"Gran told me to leave you alone."

"Good job," Reggie said.

"Did you get in trouble with your coach or something?"

"Apparently."

"Rain's mom gave me her extra popcorn tonight."

He snorted. "At least the game wasn't a total loss."

"Did Mom and Dad use to get grumpy a lot?"

"Why do you ask?"

"Just making sure it's not a genetic thing I need to watch out for."

"Always with the honesty," Reggie muttered. "I don't think so. I remember them happy, but maybe that's just what I want to remember. I wish I remembered more, even if there was bad stuff."

He left unsaid that he had tried desperately to remember some clue that his parents had known about grana. A stray book like the one Twig had found, or a quiet conversation . . . anything. But it was like searching through a fog, and when a random memory surfaced, it was a hug, or a laugh, or a silly game. Reggie had never spoken to P about the box or the note inside; he didn't see how it would help, and it seemed like a lot to share with an eight-year-old. One day, maybe.

"I wish they were here," P said.

"Me too," he replied softly.

She was quiet for a little while. Then she sat up straight and faced him.

"Want to play our game?" she asked.

"P, it's like midnight—"

"Please."

He sighed and sat up, though he couldn't help but smile. Their mom had taught him the "word game." You faced the other person and said a word. Then they had to instantly add one to the sentence, and back and forth it went until someone invariably said something silly or nonsensical. He and P used to play it all the time, and they always tried to make each other the subject of some ridiculous sentence. It was a race to get the other one's name in first, so it was forbidden to start with a name. They had to begin with something else and work up to the name.

She cleared her throat. "There—"

"Was—" he replied.

"A—"

"Girl—"

"Named—"

He smiled at the win. "P—"

She giggled. "Who—"

"Was—"

"A—"

"Very—"

"Brilliant—" she said, smiling.

"But—"

P opened her mouth, paused, then frowned at him. "How does that work?"

"I was thinking: a very brilliant but annoying little sister."

P laughed and smacked his arm. "Again?"

"Last one. If Gran finds us both awake, we'll be cleaning all weekend."

"We'll probably be cleaning all weekend anyway, but fine. You first."

He thought for a second. "The—"

"Boy—" she said pointedly.

"From—"

"The—"

"Bottom—" he said, snorting.

"Lost—"

He frowned. "His—"

"Way—"

Reggie fell silent, his mind slipping back to the game. "Yeah," he said quietly.

"Yeah?" she said. "That doesn't work. I was thinking: And laid a trail of bread crumbs—"

"I think that was a good ending already," he cut in. "Come on. Bed."

P glared at him, then wrapped him in a quick hug and started for the door.

"Reggie?" she said, turning back at the doorway.

"Yeah?"

"That would be a terrible ending."

POOL PARTY PLANS

We are not inspired by success.
We are inspired by the triumph over adversity.

◆ WIZENARD ◇60◇ PROVERB ◆

THE NEXT MORNING, Reggie boarded the first of three buses to connect him a mere twenty miles to the suburban north—the only somewhat respectable area of the Bottom. The region was basically split into its four directional sections: the industrial south, home to factories, mines, and the majority of available jobs; the west and east, which were both impoverished; and the comparatively wealthy suburban north, where any Bottom residents who had even a little money congregated and separated themselves from the rest.

He had driven here once or twice with Gran, though it was still strange to see grass again, and nice homes, and working cars. It was nothing like the areas outside the Bottom—they got to see that lavish, alien landscape every away game—but it was a *very* big step up from Swain Street.

He was strangely nervous about today. Not about going to a

nice part of town or pools or anything of the sort—he realized he was anxious about seeing his teammates. He had worked all week and been benched the entire game. Maybe the team had wanted that. Maybe they had all decided Reggie was better left on the bench after his disastrous start to the season. The thought hurt, but it wouldn't surprise him. Reggie wondered if the team was really better off without him.

At least Twig will want me here, he thought miserably. *I hope.*

Stepping off the third and final bus, he followed Twig's directions for a couple of blocks, forcing smiles at the residents who seemed to have some sort of internal alarm that an outsider had wandered into their midst. It certainly didn't help his trepidation.

Reggie made it to Twig's house a few minutes later and stopped in front of the driveway, awed. He knew Twig was from the north end. He didn't know he lived . . . *here*. The house was huge. The walls were a mixture of brick and white slatted siding, free of weathering and graffiti unlike every building in the West Bottom. A spotless asphalt driveway bore two rust-free cars, and best of all, near the garage hung a brand-new basketball net with a huge glass backboard.

Reggie stared at it longingly. The hoop was beautiful . . . even better than the ones at Fairwood.

It all seemed closer to a palace than a home, but the neighbors' homes were the same, like an entire street of kings and queens from Gran's old stories. Reggie looked down at himself for a moment. Basketball shorts devolving to thread. His dad's crispy leather boots. He had even brought a plastic grocery bag with some muffins. He felt a bit ridiculous about them now, but Gran had insisted it was polite. He took a deep, shaky breath and rang the oddly musical doorbell.

Twig swung the door open, grinning.

"Five minutes to noon," Twig said. "I figured you'd be first."

"Is that okay?" Reggie asked uncertainly.

"Yeah! Come in. What's in the bag?"

"I . . . uh . . . well, Gran said it was polite to bring something."

Reggie fished a little sandwich bag out with six fresh oatmeal muffins inside.

"Thanks," Twig said, taking them and starting down the hall. "Gran's finest?"

Reggie snorted. "If I baked them, we could use them for baseballs."

"Good to know," Twig said, laughing. "Backyard is this way."

Reggie followed him, taking in the dining room and living room and entering a big kitchen overlooking the yard. More grass out there, and bushes, and a big square pool in the center with lounge chairs around it. Twig's father hovered over a barbecue in the corner, wearing an apron and turning hot dogs and burgers.

"Hello, Reggie," Twig's mother said, cutting vegetables at the counter.

Two parents. Of all the things he had seen so far, he longed for that the most.

"Hello, Mrs. Zetz," he replied, exactly as Gran had instructed. "Thank you for having me over."

"Our pleasure! You want something to drink? Juice?"

"Yes, please. Thank you."

Gran had said to be extra polite, so he was basically pulling out everything at once. He followed Twig outside with his fruit juice and sat in one of the lounge chairs beside the pool.

"You . . . always live here?" Reggie asked.

"Pretty much," Twig said. "We moved from a few blocks over when I was little."

"It's really nice."

Twig smiled, though he looked distinctly uncomfortable. "I hope the guys don't . . . mind."

"What do you mean?"

"It was my dad's idea to do this. He suggested it last season too. Like, every week."

"He did?" Reggie asked incredulously.

"Yeah. I always said no."

Reggie looked at the clear, beautiful pool. He could smell the meat on the grill. *"Why?"*

Twig shifted again, glancing at his dad. "I know things are different in the West Bottom. I mean, I go there all the time now. I was trying to fit in. I didn't think this would help."

Reggie considered that. It was true enough—Twig was living a very different life from anyone else on the team. Even more than the others had guessed. Vin's family was the wealthiest of the rest, but his house was nothing like Twig's, and it was still in the destitute West Bottom.

This place was different. The green everywhere. The space. The feel of it.

He realized Twig was watching him, and he understood why

Twig had been so happy to see Reggie arrive first. Twig was obviously worried about the others, and he wanted to see how his closest friend on the team reacted. Reggie felt a pang of sympathy. It seemed they were both worried about what the rest of the team was thinking. At least Twig was actually contributing.

But he really did look concerned, so Reggie clapped him on the shoulder.

"You're a Badger, Twig," he said. "Doesn't matter where you live. And trust me—the guys are going to be focused on those hot dogs and veggies and watching Big John try to swim."

Twig laughed. "I got my mom to grab some water wings."

"No you didn't."

Twig ran to the shed and came back holding up two pink inflatable water wings.

Reggie burst out laughing. "Now, this will be good."

The team filed in over the next hour. Reggie watched them a bit nervously, but no one seemed to do anything but nod or give him props. It could have been pity, he supposed. Peño arrived on crutches, his foot in a cast, with Rain and Lab flanking him on either side like bodyguards. They settled him into a poolside recliner, and Peño leaned back, sighing.

"My first pool party and I can't even swim," Peño said.

"How does the ankle feel?" Twig asked.

"Numb," he said. "Thank goodness Pops put some money aside. Cost a fortune just to get this piñata put on my foot." He patted Lab's shoulder. "Lab is going to have to start eating dirt."

"We'll be fine," Lab said. "Just try to be less clumsy."

"I'm out for the season, probably," Peño said. "Could be back for nationals, maybe."

Lab snorted. "Nationals? We're O and five."

"For now," Peño agreed. "We got to make some changes. Seven games left."

Reggie wasn't sure if he imagined it, but he thought Rain and Peño shared a quick nod. He almost chewed a nail. Had they found a new player? Maybe two . . . one for Peño and one for Reggie. If they had managed to find some talent, maybe they figured they could still go on a run.

"Welcome, boys!" Twig's father said when the whole team had gathered. "Tough start to the year, of course. But you'll get there. I actually had some ideas, and I did invite that coach—"

There were a few snickers around the team.

"I don't think he's much of a pool party guy, Mr. Zetz," Peño said.

Mr. Zetz nodded. "That's what he said. But he does seem to know his ball. I should know. Played a bit myself. A real force down low. Remind me to show you my trophies later—"

"Dad!" Twig said.

"Later," his dad said quickly. "Food, anyone?"

The team rushed the grill. Reggie wondered if Twig knew that most of them had never seen so much food in one place. Beef was rare and much more expensive than pork, and Big John ate six burgers at least and was soon shuffling around with a hand clenched over his belly.

Reggie eventually stripped off his socks and sat on the edge of the pool, dangling his feet into the cool water. He felt strangely lonely in the crowded yard, like an outsider who had wandered into a team party and would be thrown out again at any moment. He looked down at his reflection and thought back to the first game of the season, when Rolabi told him he was first off the bench.

For the second time, he had really thought things were going to change.

And, for the second time, he had been wrong.

"There was only pink?" a loud voice asked suspiciously.

Twig was showing Big John the water wings, trying not to laugh. "That's it."

Big John stared at them for a minute, and then pulled off his shirt. "Well, if you are all too cowardly to go swimming, I'll show you how it's done." He pulled on the water wings, squeezing them around his thick arms, and eyed them dubiously. "You think these will work?"

"How many burgers you eat again?" Peño asked.

Big John sighed. "Here goes nothing."

With that, he took a running jump into the pool, shouting: "Baaaaaadgerrrrrrs!"

He hit belly first with a sharp *clap*, spraying everyone with water. Reggie shook with laughter as Big John surfaced and half swam, half splashed toward the shallow end, all frantic kicking and pink water wings thrashing about.

After that, everyone climbed into the shallow end, including Reggie. He even took a turn with some floats out in the deeper water—his first ever attempt at swimming. Twig attempted to coach him, but when Reggie tried to imitate his moves, he found he was doing way more splashing than swimming. But even that didn't distract him for long. He kept seeing Rain and Peño exchanging looks, as if they were coordinating something. Rain was also moving around the group, talking to each player in turn in low voices. As the hours wore on, Reggie was sure Rain had gone to every single player . . . except for Reggie. New players . . . it had to be.

Reggie just waited for the bad news, feeling his stomach somewhere in his toes.

He went to the bathroom, and when he returned, he saw the whole team gathered around Peño's lounge chair, all wrapped up in towels and drying in the sun. His stomach sank further. Now they were having a full team meeting without him?

He shuffled over to join the team, staying on the edge, trying to pick up the conversation. But it was dead silent, and as one, the whole team turned to him, separating enough that Peño could stare up at him, wearing a strange, knowing smile. Rain stepped out as well, grinning.

"What's up?" Reggie asked slowly.

"Rain and I were talking this morning," Peño said. "About you."

Reggie felt his stomach settle in the Earth's core. He'd been right. They were going to ask him to quit. Reggie tried to keep his face straight, waiting for them to continue.

He should have known this was coming, but it stung worse than he'd imagined.

"And?" he finally managed.

"We need to make some changes," Peño said. "I suggested you move to point."

Reggie looked around, waiting for someone to laugh. "What?"

"You know all the plays. You have handles. I thought you would be a good fit."

"I agreed," Twig said, grinning. "We all did."

Reggie felt a flutter of hope. *Point?* Did that mean they wanted him to start playing more?

"Except for me," Rain interjected. "I thought it would be a mistake."

The hope fluttered away again. Rain was the best player and the team leader. And these days, he was also very honest. If Rain thought Reggie didn't have it, then they would all agree.

"I said you were a shooting guard," Rain said. "And had a shot to be great. I know it's been a rough season. But we see you in practice. When you are going, you dominate, man."

Reggie frowned. "Well, I do play shooting guard. Behind you, remember?"

"I do," Rain said, finally revealing a smile. "Not anymore. I'm moving to point."

Reggie was sure they were joking now. Rain was their star player. Their leading scorer.

"Very funny—" Reggie started.

"He talked us into it," Peño said. "He does know the plays too. And he likes to pass now, apparently. I said Rolabi must have hypnotized him or thrown him off a mountain or something."

"I think I can help move the offense from there," Rain continued. "But we need firepower from the two spot. We need a guard who can take over the play and lock it down on defense."

"And you thought of me?" Reggie asked, stunned. "Rolabi wants me to quit!"

Twig laughed. "No he doesn't. He's pushing you. I don't think *you* see it sometimes, but when you get in the zone, the ball goes through you, Reg. We know you can take the next step."

Reggie looked at them, stunned. "I lost us the game three weeks ago. And then was suspended, and then benched the next one. Have you guys been watching the same season?"

"You've had a tough start . . . no doubt about that," Rain said. "But you've been crushing it in practice lately, dude. And we think you can *win* us games. We need you out on the floor."

Cash laid a big hand on his shoulder.

"Time to let out the beast," he said quietly.

Reggie fumbled for the words, then settled on a murmured "Thanks, guys."

"I want to see the player who knocked me on my butt at practice," Rain said. "That Reggie doesn't like to lose, and neither do I. If we're going to have any chance of making the nationals, we can't lose another game."

"It's true," Vin said, nodding. "We need to win seven straight for sure."

Reggie paused. "What about Rolabi—"

"I think he'll support our decision," Peño said. "Leave the big man to us."

"Or he'll tie us into pretzels," Lab added.

"Let's turn it around next week," Rain said, putting his hand in. "Let's get it going."

"Badgers on three?" Peño said. "One . . . two . . . three . . ."

"Badgers!"

They all broke apart, laughing, and Twig swung an arm over Reggie's shoulders.

"Bet you didn't see that coming?" he asked.

"I've never been more surprised in my life," Reggie said. "And I have Rolabi Wizenard for a basketball coach." He shook his head. "I just hope I can live up to all this. I don't know."

"I do," Twig said. "But it wasn't me. It was all Rain. That guy *believes* in you."

Reggie glanced back at Rain, who was talking with Peño again. "Well, it means a lot."

"It should," Twig agreed. "One of the best shooting guards in Dren gave up his position for you. Not because he wants to play point. It's because he thinks you're going to be better."

Reggie felt the weight of that sink in. It seemed preposterous. But he had to try.

"Crush it this week," Twig said, tapping Reggie's chest. "No more losses."

"I'm going to try," Reggie said.

Twig grinned. "You need to do more than that. You need to help us win."

"I've been on the bench for three years, man. I'm not going to suddenly be a star—"

"No," Twig said. "You already are one. You just haven't realized it yet."

Reggie didn't know what to say to that. He wanted to argue. He also kind of wanted to give him a hug. But he decided he didn't need to reply. He just needed to prove them right.

Reggie stuck his arm out and gave Twig props. "Thanks for having me today, man."

Twig frowned. "The party isn't over. Hey, where you going?"

Reggie had already started for the patio doors. He glanced over his shoulder.

"Back to work."

DO YOU

Struggle is the training of the soul.

❖ WIZENARD ⟨69⟩ PROVERB ❖

REGGIE WALKED INTO the gym two and a half hours later, sweat-stained, exhausted, and still plastered with pollen and leaves and dirt from his shortcuts out of the north end. He'd made it all the way home and caught the bus to Fairwood. Gran hadn't even asked where he was going.

She'd taken one look at him from the couch and waved her arm in permission before rolling over again. Lying on the couch during the day was very unusual for her, not to mention the thick sweater, but he'd assumed it was just an extra long week at the diner. At least she had a day off tomorrow to try and catch up on some rest.

Reggie changed his shoes on the bench, relishing the silence. He was nervous, though he wasn't sure why. It was just another solo practice. But for some reason, the air felt charged today . . . like it was waiting for something.

When he was ready, he walked toward the hoop, pounding the ball in time with his steps as always. He was excited to drain some shots. He needed to see the ball go down. Then half the lights blinked out. Reggie's shadow stretched out across the floor, and he had enough foresight to jump back as the shadow rose.

"Figured you'd be here," Reggie said. "You're part of grana, obviously. So are you here to help? The parrot did, eventually. And the sticky floor. But so far you're kind of a jerk."

His shadow just stood there. In truth, Reggie was talking to himself more than anyone.

"So what's the lesson? What are *you* trying to teach me?"

He dribbled the ball methodically through his legs.

"Right. Well, I guess I have to beat you to find out."

He tried a quick, half-hearted fake to the right and was promptly bodychecked. He flew onto his tailbone, sending a lance of pain up his back, and then rolled away in surprise as his shadow tried to stomp on him. Reggie pushed himself up, searching for his ball.

It was now sitting behind the shadow, about twenty feet away.

"What is wrong with you?" he shouted.

Naturally, his shadow didn't reply. It just got low, blocking the way to the ball.

"This isn't a lesson! I have a game Friday. I need to play better. Help me!"

His voice leapt around the gym, echoing again and again, getting louder instead of quieter, and changing slowly as before, a single word at a time, until all he could hear was:

Do I want this, do I want this, do I want this—

"Stop that!" Reggie said.

He tried another fake and was hit again. This time his body twisted in midflight, and he landed face-first, his cheek smacking off the hardwood with enough force to rattle teeth. He stared sideways at the gym for a moment, dazed, then stood, listening to the now-fading words:

Do you want this, do you want this, do you—

"Yes!" he shouted.

He turned to the shadow. It looked taller than him, somehow. Broader. Stronger. Didn't everyone? His shadow was clearly waiting for another fake, crouching and primed on its toes.

It didn't get a fake this time.

Reggie charged directly at the shadow, shoulder down, and plowed right into its midsection. Then he started to *push*. The shadow slid back, fighting desperately for balance, soon equaling him in strength. But Reggie drove one foot after the other, pushing the shadow back toward center court. His legs ached with the strain. One slow, steady step. Then another.

Do you, do you, do you—

With a last explosion of effort, Reggie shoved the shadow back and dove atop the basketball, gathering it to his stomach like he was protecting a baby. He lay with it huddled in his arms, curled up, panting, and waiting to be attacked. But Fairwood was empty again, and he rolled onto his back and stared at the ceiling, still panting, completely spent. All the fluorescent panels were fully lit. The echo was gone; maybe for good. He clearly wanted to be a baller. That was obvious.

Was that the test with his shadow? How many times did he have to prove his desire?

Deep down, he suspected he was missing something.

He stopped at the statue on the way home. He stared at it, feeling the same hatred as always. The same loss. It wasn't just that his parents were gone. It was that they had been *taken*. It was that this man could take them and live his life and have statues built of him, and Reggie had to sit and watch. His parents' murder had bored a hole through him, and it was still growing, draining him.

He began to chuck rocks at the figure again, feeling a grim satisfaction as one after another pinged off the bronze. Finally, he sat down on the curb. The statue loomed over him still. He thought back to Gran's words. To his "festering wound."

She was wrong. It felt good to blame Talin, and *right*, no matter how many times Gran said otherwise. Vaguely, he knew he didn't have proof. But he knew it in his gut. He *would* prove it.

"I suppose we all have our hobbies."

Reggie started and turned to find Rolabi standing beside him, gazing up at the statue.

"Oh, Professor. I . . . didn't see you."

"You didn't think I existed outside of the gym, did you?"

Reggie paused. "It crossed my mind."

"Well, I live far from here, so don't be too alarmed. But tonight I felt like taking a walk." He glanced down at Reggie. "The Bottom is far from Argen, but there are always eyes watching."

Reggie flushed and looked away. "Professor . . . can I ask you something?"

"You can."

"What is grana? How does it really work? Is it possible my mother knew about it?"

Rolabi stood there for a moment, still studying the statue. "All of us know grana, or at least the possibility of grana, whether we realize it or not. And for each of us it is different. It is always a reflection of self."

"You must have written that book Twig found," Reggie muttered.

"It is natural to wish to know all, to understand all, immediately. The unknown is uncomfortable. But the patient search for knowledge, the reward of discovering it oneself, is important. Be careful in creating your own knowledge to explain the unknown, Reggie. It may be misleading."

"My mother left me something—"

"Then she left it for you. To find meaning in for yourself." Rolabi turned to him. "I advise you not to return here to throw stones. You hurt yourself far more than you hurt him."

Rolabi started across the intersection, moving quickly with his long, smooth strides.

"Sir, the team met today—"

"I will see you Monday at practice," Rolabi said without looking back. "Be ready."

Reggie shot a final, hateful glare at the statue and started home. As he did, he reflected on Rolabi's words, and one line in particular: *It is always a reflection of self.* That wasn't in either of the books—the textbook or the children's story—and it nagged at him. It felt important.

When he got home, he showered and crawled into bed, feeling the ache across his body.

"Well, Mom and Dad," he said quietly, "I think this is going to be quite the week."

ENOUGH

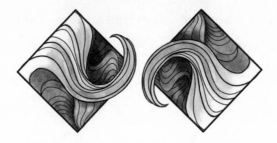

Compromise is a part of life. But not when it comes to dreams.
For those, one must seek the stars or nothing.

✦ WIZENARD ◆58◆ PROVERB ✦

YOU SAW ROLABI outside of the gym?" Twig said incredulously. "I kind of thought—"

"He only existed here?" Reggie said. "I know."

They were shooting around before Monday practice, and Reggie had pulled him aside to relate the strange encounter. He told him what Rolabi said as well, emphasizing the one line about reflecting the self.

"Makes sense to me," Twig said. "The reflection part, anyway."

Twig had alluded to some sort of vision about mirrors during training camp, but never elaborated further, and Reggie didn't press him on it. From what he could tell, his teammates had each experienced some sort of deeper vision when they caught their orbs—Twig said it was basically the center of his fear. Reggie had gotten no such vision, just a flash of his parents far away.

"I guess if we play our best, grana will be good?" Twig said.

"Maybe," Reggie said. "But I don't need help if I'm already playing good. There must be something else. I couldn't control it with words or thoughts. So, maybe it's something else."

"Like what?"

Reggie sighed. "I have no idea. I brought your book back, by the way."

Twig shook his head. "You keep it. Do us all a favor and figure out how grana works."

Rolabi strode through the doors of the gym and waited until the full team had gathered in front of him at center court.

"We are O and five," Rolabi said. "Three teams in the conference are already five and O, including the Titans. We are unlikely to catch any of them, but four teams go to the playoffs. Two more teams are currently three and two . . . a significant head start. We have seven games left. What does this all mean?"

"It means we can't lose again," Rain said quietly.

Lab nodded. "If we want to go to the playoffs, we need to win out."

Reggie saw a few players shift, looking dubious. Winning seven straight games would be hard enough . . . but they still had some of the top teams in the conference remaining on their schedule. Just this Friday they were traveling to Milton to play the southeast conference's biggest star, Oren Laithe, and the defending champion Marauders. They were a "super team," of the southeast conference's best players—recruited basically as toddlers—of which Oren was the brightest prospect of all. They had placed fourth in the *nationals*. It was the hardest matchup of the year.

"Super," Big John said.

"Unlikely," Rolabi replied. "Unless we believe we can. Without doubt. Without fear."

Reggie turned to the banners on the north wall. Decades of Bottom teams . . . and not one had ever made it to the nationals. Not even *one*. A divisional runner-up before the new open system had been implemented was the all-time record, and that was only good for seventh place in the overall conference. The Badgers were trying to do the impossible, and they were starting from an 0-5 hole. It seemed even beyond the reach of dreams. And they were counting on him.

If Rolabi agreed.

"Starting this Friday, every game is a must-win. Every half. Every quarter. Every possession is a must-win. It won't be easy, and any victories will start with sweat. Laps. Go."

"Professor?" Rain said. "We would like to suggest a change."

Reggie felt his stomach clench. This was it. How would the professor react?

Rolabi turned to him. "Do not suggest. Present."

"I would like to move to point," Rain replied. "I believe I can be effective there. And we all agreed that Reggie is ready to step in at the two. It's a big backcourt, and we can both score."

Reggie glanced at Rolabi, fighting the urge to chew his nails. Some coaches might take offense to lineup suggestions . . . especially for a player he had just benched. Would he get mad? What would that even look like? Rolabi scanned the team, then turned at last to Reggie.

"Good," he said at last. "But even a great plan will take us nowhere without work. Laps."

Reggie let out a breath. He was getting his shot . . . and he wasn't sure if it was making him more or less nervous now. It didn't really matter. Today, he just had to work. The team started around the gym, and Reggie fell in beside Rain. The Badgers' newest point guard looked over and grinned.

"Ready?" Rain asked.

"I think so," Reggie replied.

Rain clapped his chest. "No thinking required, bro," he said. "Just let it out."

"Listen, I just wanted to say thanks—"

"Thank me by playing hard on Friday," Rain said.

The team slowed after twenty laps—by now they all knew they had to each hit a free throw to move on—and Rolabi threw a ball to Reggie. The professor's face was completely expressionless.

"One free throw can win games," he said. "And one can lose them."

Reggie walked out to the free-throw line. He felt his nervousness growing with every step. He stepped up to the line and took a deep breath. The hoop was small again—far too small to score on. Reggie felt a flare of panic and tried to relax, dribbling the ball slowly to find his rhythm. If grana really was a reflection of self, then panic probably wouldn't help.

Sure enough, the hoop grew with each breath, like he was inflating a balloon.

Before today, he had mostly thought about letting himself down. Now the team had put their trust in him. They'd told him they believed in him. He felt the pressure of that creep in.

What if I blow my chance? What if the fog comes back Friday?

What if I let them down?

His throat dried up. His chest tightened. The calm fled.

When Reggie put up the shot, the hoop was barely big enough to slide a pin through. The ball bounced away, and he heard a groan from the team. They would have to run five more laps now. Reggie ran back to join them, and the doubts swirled, and the laps grew harder. Every direction was uphill. His shoes felt like cinder blocks. Five short laps soon felt like five hundred.

When they stopped, Rolabi threw him the ball again.

"All talk of winning and plans means nothing. One must face the moment."

Reggie managed a nod and walked to the free-throw line. The hoop was fluctuating again. Small to large. Ten feet away, then twenty. The ball seemed to grow heavier with every dribble.

He missed the shot. Then another.

When he walked up the fourth time, the whole gym seemed to be going mad. The floorboards were warped. The hoop was tiny. The ball was a gray stone.

He lifted the ball, knowing even before he shot it that the pressure was too much.

Grana is a reflection of self. He repeated the words. There was no point in shooting now, so he dribbled the ball, breathing in and out. He didn't try to command grana or ask it to change. He just let the anxiety fade away and inhaled deeply, and the hoop began to grow.

He thought about their exercise with the daisy—they still did it twice a week. They just sat and watched it grow, focusing on the details, letting time *slow*. He did the same with the rim.

Then he slowly rose up and drained the free throw.

"Live in the moment and you will never miss it," Rolabi said quietly. "Two-on-ones. We'll need transition baskets against the stout Marauders defense. They are well organized in the half-court, and so we must be ready to run." He turned to Reggie. "Reggie, you start on defense."

Reggie barely had time to run down the court and turn around before the two attackers were on him. It was a drill designed to work on passing and finishing at the rim—the defender had little chance of stopping two players unless they made a blatant mistake.

Rain and Twig didn't, and after a quick give-and-go, Rain easily laid the ball in.

Reggie prepared to swap in as an attacker and transition the other way with Twig. The attacker who scored—Rain in this case—stayed back on defense, while the remaining two charged back up the court to take on a new waiting defender and so forth.

"The defender stays," Rolabi said loudly. "He stays until he has ten stops."

"Coach—" Rain said.

"Ten stops," Rolabi repeated.

Reggie frowned and got into his stance. Ten stops was a lot in this drill—he had seen it go a hundred times without a miss. What was Rolabi playing at? Was he offended by their suggestion? Was he trying to prove that Reggie didn't have what it took? Heat rushed to his cheeks. If that's what Rolabi was after, he was going to be disappointed. Reggie was ready.

"Come on, then," he whispered.

The drill started again. One wave of attackers after another swept toward him, using give-and-go plays, lob passes, or just pure brute strength to get past him and score again and again. He was crossed by Rain so badly that he tripped. He was sent flying by a Cash pivot on the block. Twig actually dunked on him after a lob, leading to yet more cheers, though he did apologize.

"Don't say sorry," Rain interjected. "Do it again. Do it until he stops you."

Reggie just nodded and turned to face the next wave. "I got this."

He refocused. He stayed on his toes and kept his back straight and managed to grind out a few stops. But it was hard. It was two-on-one every time, and he could only do so much. Soon, Reggie had faced 100 attacks. Then 150. He stopped counting.

After what seemed like hours, Reggie had accumulated nine stops, most from missed jumpers when the attackers got bored of taking it to the hoop. But the ninth had been ages ago, and no matter how hard he tried, he couldn't get the tenth and a merciful end to the drill. It seemed to be getting harder. Sometimes the floor slanted against him. Once, he ran into an invisible wall. At another point he forgot about his footwork, and his feet sank into the floorboards.

"That's enough!" he whispered after Cash laid one in. "That's enough."

It was like every gift came with an attached punishment: He filled in for Rain, and the gym filled with fog. He worked harder than ever for a week, and he sat on the bench. He got named a starter by the team, and now Rolabi was trying to break him. The world refused to let him stand.

Reggie doubled over as the next two attackers charged down

the floor: Jerome and Lab. More sweat poured onto the hard-wood. His hands shook on his wobbling knees. It was enough.

Reggie lifted his head, seeing Jerome and Lab approach through the haze of sweat. He watched as they passed the ball back and forth. Felt the vibrations in the maple slats. Tasted salt on his lips. They were confident. Careless. Jerome threw it to Lab, Lab threw it back, and Jerome went in for the easy layup. But Reggie had been waiting for the obvious play.

He threw himself across the block, swatting the ball and col-liding with Jerome in the process. Jerome hit the ground, staring up at Reggie in surprise as the ball bounced away.

Reggie stared back at him, hands clenched. *"Ten."*

"Water break," Rolabi said.

Reggie pulled Jerome up, and Jerome grinned. "Bring that out on Friday, boy."

"I told you: he's a *dog* when he's angry!" Big John said, laughing.

Reggie started for the bench, slowly letting his hands unclench. That had been even more intense than his drill with Rain. He had simply decided that he would not be scored on again. It had over-whelmed his doubts and his fatigue and all those anxious thoughts swirling around: the decision to *win*. It was like a raging current. If you chose to win, truly, you had to be all in. Reggie downed his water bottle in one protracted gulp. That mind-set was what he needed.

The rest of the practice wasn't any easier. If Reggie made any errors, Rolabi let him know. He was isolated on defense and swarmed on O. He collided with picks. He was forced to fight down low on the block. Called out for every miss.

When it ended, Reggie plopped onto the bench, so tired that

he could barely change his shoes. Twig dropped down beside him.

"Well, that was intense," Twig said.

Reggie frowned. "Rolabi does not like the idea of me playing."

"I agree."

"You do? Why didn't you say something—"

"Rolabi doesn't want you to play," Twig said. "He wants you to *win*."

Reggie looked up. "By kicking my butt all day?"

"Exactly."

"You should be a Wizenard in training."

Twig grinned. "I am definitely wise enough. The suit is the problem. Couldn't wear it all day."

"The more I get to know you, the weirder you become."

"Thank you," Twig said gravely. He gave Reggie props. "Nice work. More tomorrow."

"I can barely walk."

Twig started for the door, then turned back and put on his deepest voice. "One must walk before one can run. Or something like that."

The rest of the team filed out, leaving Reggie alone in his soggy shoes.

"Well, grana," he said, "looks like I'm a starter. But we still have a long way to go."

His own words echoed around the gym for a moment, and he sighed.

"Right."

He scooped up his ball and started shooting.

BELOW THE BOTTOM

The deeper the hole, the longer the climb,
and the stronger you arrive.

◆ WIZENARD ◆ 68 ◆ PROVERB ◆

EARLY THE NEXT morning, Reggie listened as Gran got ready for work, coughing while she made her coffee. She had coughed before bed as well, and looked a little tired, but he should have known she would be up and out the door by seven as always. He lay there for a while longer, trying to fall back asleep. But his mind was restless, eager for more, so he climbed out of bed to go make breakfast.

When he was finished, he left for Fairwood, slinging his duffel bag over his shoulders and hurrying down the concrete steps. The sun was low as he walked, casting a red glow over the Bottom. It almost looked as if the city were on fire. Reggie found himself practicing his jab steps as he walked, and then he took his ball out and started to dribble down the sidewalk, sending deep drumbeats down the alleyways. He had three days left until the showdown with Oren Laithe and the Milton

Marauders. Three days to change the season. Three days to change everything.

When he arrived, he changed quickly and started shooting. He went to the corner first, then the mid-range, hitting both far more consistently. As he worked his way back out to the top of the key, he realized he could still see the hoop. Grana was finally letting him shoot from somewhere else. As he moved into the low post, he started working on turnaround jumpers—a quick pivot and straight into a shot. But as he spun, a jagged wooden stalagmite suddenly leapt from the ground, spearing the ball as it left his fingers. Reggie gasped and stumbled back.

"What the . . . ?" he said. "My ball!"

Before he could pluck the deflated ball from the stalagmite, the jagged shape retracted into the floor. Reggie's ball bounced off the flat hardwood, undamaged. He ran his hands over the pebbling protectively. Frowning, he tried another turnaround, and once again, a jutting hardwood fragment shot out and punctured the ball with a sickening *pop*.

This time, Reggie studied the stalagmite. He realized that it rose up just a few inches above his release—six at most. He needed to figure this out.

Once again, he reached for the ball, the stalagmite disappeared, and the ball became whole again. Reggie bit his lip, thinking. He had been blocked a few times in the post last practice. Actually, a lot of times. Reggie had a very regimented release—he liked to go straight up and keep his body upright. It was good form, but maybe that wasn't always the best strategy when he was being guarded down low. Maybe he needed more space. How could he find some?

Reggie turned his back to the net, spun right, and faked a jumper. As he expected, another stalagmite leapt out, but he whirled back the other way, hoping to find his space. Instead, a second spike burst out of the floor, and he faded back out of reflex. The ball *just* made it over the top of the wooden spike, but it fell short of the rim. His backward momentum had thrown it off.

"Fadeaways," Reggie said, nodding. "Not my specialty. Well, I guess that's the point."

He spent the next few hours working on his low-post game, spinning into fadeaways to get the ball over the jutting wooden shards. Sometimes three or four leapt out in response to his fakes and extra steps, but always, he bought an extra few inches by fading back on the release.

At first, he missed the majority. He realized he needed more strength from his wrists and fingers to make up for the change in angle—he couldn't power the shot from legs that were busy moving *away* from the net. So he slowly adjusted the mechanics and found his range until he hit more than he missed. Reggie knew it would take hundreds of hours to get where he needed to be.

But it was a start.

When he got home that night, they had a quiet dinner—apart from Gran's sniffles and coughing—and he went to bed early, hoping for a quick practice before school the next day.

But Reggie woke the next morning to violent coughing. He immediately rolled out of bed and hurried to the living room, where Gran was lying on the couch, swaddled in two blankets and still trembling. Her usual morning coffee lay cold and mostly untouched beside her on the carpet.

"Didn't want to keep waking P," she said.

"*Gran*," he breathed, crouching down beside her to feel her head. "You're burning up."

"Head cold. I already took some cough syrup. Need to get up soon for work . . ."

"Head colds don't usually come with a fever," he cut in. "You need a doctor."

She sputtered. "A *what*? We can't even afford to look at a doctor, boy. I'm fine—" She was interrupted by another violent coughing fit. Her body writhed through it. "It's just a little bug."

"I'm calling the diner," he said, heading for the phone.

"I can work—"

"No," Reggie said firmly. "You have to rest."

She glared at him, then nodded. "Tell them I'll make it up Sunday."

Her manager, Ron, made a bit of a stink—he really was awful—but Reggie insisted and said he would call tomorrow morning if she wasn't any better. He said that part very quietly.

When he hung up, he went to get her some more water.

"I'll stay home today—"

"You most certainly will not," she said. "I need sleep. And we do not skip school."

"Gran—"

"Nonnegotiable," she said, and then proceeded to cough again. Reggie just shook his head and got everything set up for her—a glass of water, a few crackers and a slice of buttered bread, and another blanket. She waved him away.

"Thank you. Now get ready. And wake that sister of yours. Poor thing."

Thirty minutes later, Reggie took a last look at Gran as he shut the door. Color continued to leach from her cheeks like a pen draining ink.

"I've never seen Gran so sick," P said.

"I know," Reggie said, leading her down the stairs. "It's just a cold."

"What do we do if she gets really sick?" P asked.

They stepped out into the morning, and Reggie didn't answer her.

He had no idea.

After school ended, Reggie hurried home with P and found Gran sleeping fitfully. Her forehead felt a little cooler, and her cough had abated, but she was still very weak and sweating profusely.

Reggie got dinner ready, then cleaned up the kitchen, worrying the whole time. But he was also keenly aware of the time. He had never missed a practice before . . . and this really wasn't a good day to start, right after the team had shown so much faith in him. He had to show Rolabi he deserved a shot. Reggie started chewing on his fingernail, thinking.

"One more nibble and I'll put a muzzle on you," Gran whispered.

Reggie crouched down, hand to her forehead. "I have practice, but I can stay—"

"No."

"It's not a good time," he said. "I'll go tomorrow."

Reggie realized he was nervous about today's practice. He had a lot to live up to, and he wasn't sure he could. It was easier when no one expected anything from you. He could never disappoint anyone that way. Well . . . except for himself. He had been doing that for a long time.

"The only thing you're doing here is chewing fingernails. And I feel a little better."

Reggie hesitated. "I should stay."

"P is here," she managed. "Go. Show him you are ready."

"I already tried that last week—"

"Then show him again."

Reggie knelt there for a moment. "Okay. I'll be back soon," he said, forcing a smile.

"I'll watch her, Reg," P added.

Reggie tucked Gran's blankets in, shaking his head. "You need a doctor."

"I also need a million dollars," she replied. "One is as likely as the other."

He sighed, planted a kiss on her cheek, and gestured for P to follow him to the door. He slung his duffel over his shoulder and put on his boots, guilt wrestling with the reality that he could do nothing here. Reggie didn't want to admit it, but he was scared. Gran was their mom and dad and grandparents wrapped into one, and they would be lost without her. He hadn't felt such raw fear in a long time, and he needed ball right now. He needed to sweat and ache and burn it all away.

Seeing the worry on her face, he wrapped P in a hug.

"Gran's tougher than dirt," he said firmly. "See you in a bit . . . and do your homework."

"Are you serious—" P started.

"Bye!"

He hurried down the hall, smiling as P's rant was cut off by the closing door. But that smile soon faded. Gran was sick, and there was nothing he could do. That was the grim truth of the Bottom. For all its flaws, people *could* survive here. But there was a fine balance. When something happened—a lost job, a sickness, an injury—then the floor fell out. He had seen it a hundred times before. People got swallowed up, and there was nothing below the Bottom.

But that had been his whole life. Things just happened *to* him. It had always felt like he had no control over anything. Except on the court. Out there, he could take control.

He broke out under open sky and started running for Fairwood, ready to chase it.

He arrived an hour early, facing some of his usual obstacles: disappearing rims, an antagonistic shadow, the parrot, sandbags, tilting floor . . . and he pushed through them all, fighting back cramps and aches and the little voice that said he could just *stop*.

Needing a drink, he started for the bench. Without warning, the floor tilted, and then kept going, and before long the cone had opened up again and swallowed him whole.

Reggie tumbled and slid down the hardwood embankment, plunging into darkness. As before, he slowed just before impact and found himself lying at the base of a huge cone.

He rolled onto his back. "Not this again."

Reggie climbed to his feet and realized the ball hadn't rolled in with him. Somehow, that was even more lonely. He paced around the bottom of the cone, trying to think. But there was no trick he could see. No puzzle. There was simply a hole, and him in it, and a long, impossible climb.

He gazed up at the rims, remembering his last trip down here. He had eventually given up, closed his eyes . . . quit. And it had gone away. He had been back on the same old flat ground.

But that didn't seem right now. Grana was challenging him. He couldn't just surrender.

Reggie turned and tried to sprint up the steep incline. He made it about six feet and slipped, landing hard on his chest and sliding back. He tried again. Then again. He tried to run on an angle, almost circling the slope, but with the same luck. He doubled over, panting, exhausted.

"Can't run out of here," he said. "Climbing, then."

It was more like vertical crawling. He slid upward, spreading his arms and legs wide and using bare skin to stick to the wood planks. He moved inches at a time. Minutes slipped by. Then hours. At halfway up, he glanced over his shoulder and saw a long fall below him. Then he kept climbing.

His muscles screamed with the effort. His skin burned as it slid. Every inch *hurt*.

"I won't quit," he whispered. "I deserve this. I deserve this."

As he crawled toward the distant hoops and the lights above them, he thought of all the time he had spent chasing ball. The endless practices. The nights alone in his room with rolled-up socks and a wastebasket. He loved this sport deeply. Why had it never loved him back?

He hoisted himself up another few inches, grimacing at the ache in his arms.

It made no sense. Basketball didn't choose not to love somebody. Reggie had chosen that fate for himself. He had decided he didn't deserve to be loved. Not by the parents who had died. Not by the family he couldn't seem to help. Not by the friends and teammates he kept pushing away. Not even by his beloved basketball. He looked up at the hoops hanging over the edge.

Reggie thought of the hours and days of being knocked down by his own shadow. He thought of the disappointments of his previous games, followed always by a return to the court, to get better, to try harder, to work. He thought of his love for his family and his desire to show them his greatest potential. He thought of the love and sweat and pain he had poured into this game.

And he realized now how hard he had to work to deserve that love.

"I earned this," he said. "And I'm going to keep earning it every single day."

Reggie kept climbing. And with a last gasp, he pulled himself over the edge.

He lay there for a moment, then pushed himself up just as the doors flew open.

"What up, Reggie?" Rain called. "You ready?"

He picked his ball up, nodding. "Yeah," Reggie said softly. "I am."

16

WHO WE PLAY

The one who works without boasting has twice the time to improve.
Beware the quiet contenders.

❖ WIZENARD ㊴ PROVERB ❖

REGGIE DROPPED ONTO the bench, gasping for air. It was
the night before the big game, but Rolabi wasn't taking it easy on
them. Reggie was getting it the worst, as before, but the whole
team was being ground down today. He wiped his face with his
sleeve and glanced at Jerome beside him.

"You alive?" he asked.

Jerome was staring into space, his jaw slack. "So tired," he
murmured.

"Ready for tomorrow?"

"Born ready," Jerome said, managing a smile. "If I live through
this practice, that is."

Reggie snorted and stood up. Rolabi was waiting for them at
half-court.

"We're rooting for you tomorrow, bench brother," Jerome
said, standing and stretching an arm. "Well, former bench brother.

You go now to the land of the starters. It's the bench dream."

Reggie laughed as they walked onto the court. "Starting doesn't matter to me, man. I just want to ball. Win. Play my best out there for once in my life. If it's from the bench, that's fine."

"Well, I want to be a starter," Jerome said. "Get a shot, you know? Get to a college maybe. Who knows. The guys on the bench ain't getting that. My dad tells me that every day."

"What do you mean?"

Jerome shrugged. "Just tells me I'm not going anywhere. That I'm supposed to be helping my family out of the neighborhood we're in. I don't know. He's just disappointed."

Reggie thought about that as they rejoined the group. He thought about how lucky he was to have Gran, who supported him for him . . . not for her. She gave everything and asked nothing. For some of the guys, this was their family's long-term plan: *Get rich and get us all out of here.*

"Just play for you," Reggie said. "And you'll get there."

"Winning the conference would help," Jerome said slyly.

Reggie turned back to the coach, taking a deep breath. "Yes it would."

"Tomorrow is it," Rolabi said, turning to them. "The season lives or dies tomorrow. If we lose, we will not make the nationals. No team has ever made it going six and six. We need seven straight or nothing. Every single game is now life-and-death to both our season and wider aspirations."

His eyes flashed toward Reggie.

"The world expects us to lose. It tells us to bend. We must choose our response."

Reggie thought back to Rolabi's story. The storm said "bend" to the mountain, and the mountain replied "break." Reggie smiled, finally understanding the message.

The storm was every challenge Reggie had ever encountered, every doubt that clouded his mind. The storm was the world telling him to stand aside—to admit defeat. But the mountain replied "break," implying that either the storm would break or the mountain would. The confrontation was now a life-and-death situation. All in. And in response, the storm fled before the mountain's commitment. The world was telling Reggie to bend to fate. This was his chance to reply: *Break*.

But did he have the strength?

Rain stepped out from the group and tapped his chest. "I'm ready."

"Me too," Big John said.

"Let's go!" Peño shouted from the bench. "Carry me to the playoffs, boys. Literally."

The rest of them shouted and cheered and slapped their chests. All but one. As the shouts died down, Rain turned to Reggie, who had been standing silently, lost in his own thoughts.

Rain walked up to him. "You ready?"

It was a loaded question for Reggie. How many times had he asked himself the same question in the mirror? Or before games? He thought he had been ready, and he had been disappointed.

Was this different? Had he done enough?

He met Rain's eyes. "I'll show you tomorrow."

"Wind sprints," Rolabi said loudly. "Show me now."

They launched into the wind sprints again, and Reggie

slapped the floor with each turn, pushing through his legs until they felt like jelly.

"Not one more loss!" Rain shouted, running back into line.

"Not one more!" Peño called from the bench. "Let's go!"

Reggie took off again, smacking the floorboards, letting the frustration pour out of him.

He had lost so much. And even now, the world was threatening to take more.

"Not one more," he whispered.

When practice ended, Reggie was the last to leave as usual. As he stood, his shadow appeared before him, gesturing to the floor. Reggie was tired. Sore. But he stepped onto the court anyway.

"Offense or defense?" Reggie asked, rolling his shadow the ball.

His shadow threw it back.

"All right, then," Reggie said. "Let's go."

It soon became clear that today was different. They fought for every movement. His shadow jockeyed him, swatted his arms, shoved him, elbowed him. His lip split under a hard blow.

Reggie worked harder. He was blocked and fouled, but he scored as well, and they fought mercilessly. His shadow grew ever worse: vicious and violent and cruel. He thought no opponent would ever be as malicious as the one he played now . . . this silent, faceless shadow. His shadow.

Reggie paused as he dribbled at the top of the key. *His* shadow.

He thought about all the battles he'd fought with it during training over the last few months. And was it just training? He thought back to the last games he'd played in. The doubts gnawing at his belly. The fears. The voices in his head. Every game, Reggie told himself he wasn't enough. That the chance had passed. That he didn't have it. That he would just fail again.

It's me, Reggie realized. *I've been playing against myself. In practice. In the games. Everywhere.*

He stared at the ball, thinking. The encroaching fog. The passed-up shots. The belief that someone else, *anyone else*, had to be better than him. Reggie had created that hard reality. He had chosen to live in it.

Reggie turned to his shadow and nodded. "Thank you. But it's time for me to play against someone else."

The shadow nodded back and disappeared.

When Reggie got home from practice a few hours later, P rushed over to him.

"It's worse."

He stepped around her and hurried over to Gran. She was curled into a ball, swaddled in three blankets, shivering. He knelt down beside her, pressing his hand to her forehead. It was burning hot—clearly the cough syrup had done nothing. Her eyes blinked open, watery and red, and she managed a smile, though even that seemed draining.

"How was practice?" she said.

"We need to go to the doctor—"

"You know that's not an option," she said weakly.

Reggie scowled. "We can worry about the bills later—"

"I will not saddle our family with bills," she said firmly. "Nonnegotiable."

He debated his options. He could carry her to the nearest

clinic. They could worry about the rest later. But deep down, he knew the clinic would turn them away if they came without cash in hand.

There were few clinics in the Bottom, and they were crammed and cutthroat.

Reggie sat down on the floor beside Gran and slipped his hand into hers, feeling his fingers stick against the clammy heat of her palms. P settled in next to him. They listened to Gran's raspy inhalations, like the wind through fall leaves. Reggie's heart ached.

"A good night's sleep is all I need," she whispered, closing her eyes.

He exchanged a worried look with P, then forced a smile, trying to reassure her.

"Let her get some rest," Reggie whispered. "She'll be better tomorrow."

They sat on the floor, backs against the living room chair, P leaning against his shoulder. Gran was asleep on the couch across from them. She stirred only for coughing fits, shuffling walks to the bathroom, or tiny sips of water.

It was nearly eleven and probably time for bed. But Reggie had stayed to watch over Gran, and P had joined him, and he had just draped a blanket over her. She shifted beside him, her eyes red from crying.

He had tried to tell her Gran would be fine. But P was used to disappointment.

"Agatha still giving you a hard time at school?" he asked softly.

"Sometimes."

"You still listening to her?"

She paused. "Sometimes. It was worse this week."

"What did she say?"

"The usual," P said. "It just hurts more this week."

He looked at Gran. "Yeah."

"What if something happens, Reggie?" she whispered. "We gave her the only medicine we have. If that doesn't work, what are we supposed to do?"

"It'll be fine. Trust me."

He could imagine Gran's response to that: *No matter how many times you say it . . .*

P was quiet for a moment. Then she moved closer.

"We had a race today," she murmured. "Twice around the track."

"For gym class?"

"Yeah."

"And?"

She grinned. "I won by like ten seconds. Smoked all the boys too."

"I don't doubt it for a second."

"Coach asked me about the under-sixteen team again. Said I should at least try out."

Reggie shifted to look at her. "And?"

"And I said no," she replied quickly. "But it was nice of him to ask."

Reggie leaned back again, hearing the longing in her voice. The fear of failure.

"What are you going to be when you grow up, P?" he asked.

"I don't know."

"Okay . . . what do you *think* you'll be?"

She hesitated. "I don't think I'll be anything."

He pulled her closer, feeling a ball form in his throat. She had already given up at eight years old. Reggie knew that words wouldn't change anything now. He had to *show* her that you could work for something, and bust your butt, and get it. He had to show her out on that court.

And for all the other reasons tomorrow's game mattered, that one mattered the most.

He lay on the floor in the darkness all night, listening to Gran's shallow breathing. The hours seemed endless. P was sprawled out a few feet away, sleeping soundly. It was just him and the moon. As he lay there, he made a promise to himself.

"I will change this," he whispered. "Help her through tonight, and I will fix this. This isn't our destiny. This isn't how my family falls apart. Give me tonight. I'll give them the rest."

He wasn't sure who he was talking to. Even the old gods had abandoned the Bottom.

"Please," he said as Gran's breathing slowed again. *"Please."*

He fell asleep much later, when the sky had begun to lighten.

Reggie woke to orange sunlight and instinctively turned to Gran. She was lying flat on her back, eyes closed, her whole body still. His heart squeezed, and for a moment, he couldn't move. Then her chest rose gently with the swell of breath, and he went to her side. Reggie scanned over her, noticing that her blankets were drenched . . . but cool. He laid a hand on her forehead and felt the same. Damp but cool. Desperate relief flooded through him.

"At least you got a little sleep," she said softly.

"I got lots of sleep. How do you feel?"

"You really are a bad liar," she said. "The fever broke. Sweated out. This old bird has got another day in her."

"Many days."

She smiled. "Many. Now get some rest. You can skip school for one day, I suppose."

Reggie took her hand. "That was a very long night, Gran."

"Yes," she said. "And what a beautiful morning it is now."

He smiled, and they sat there for a while, enjoying the rising sun, P still sleeping soundly on the carpet beside them. Reggie wondered about his promise. He wondered if someone had heard him.

Either way, he had a job to do.

"Big game tonight," she said. "What time does the bus leave?"

"Four. It's like a three-hour drive or something. We'll be home late."

"I can't wait to hear all about it."

He leaned against the couch. "No team from the Bottom has ever won an away game."

"Well, everything has to start somewhere."

Reggie thought about that for a moment, then stood up and started for his bedroom.

"Where you going?" she asked.

"To get my bag," Reggie said. "I was going to get another practice in."

She smiled. "Your parents would be proud, Reggie. Your mom . . . she is watching somewhere, ready for the game."

"I just hope I can make her proud," Reggie said.

"She wouldn't care if you were good, Reggie," Gran said. "She would care that you tried your hardest."

He smiled back. "Well, I can give her that, at least."

Reggie sat down with Gran and P for their very early dinner—roast chicken, rice, and beans. When Gran went to the bathroom, P stared at him.

"You all right?" P asked.

"Yeah. Why?"

She shrugged. "You seem weird."

"How so?"

"I don't know. You just do."

"I'm fine."

She frowned and went back to her dinner. "Did you find some money or—"

"What?"

"You look like you're holding in a smile."

He laughed. "I'm just excited for the game tonight."

"You . . . are?" she asked. "I don't want to be the one to say it, but—"

"I sat the entire game last week. I remember."

"So why are you excited?"

"Because it's a new week. A new game. It's exciting."

She stared at him for a moment. "Can I feel your forehead—"

"P! I'm fine." He wiped his mouth and leaned back. "Talk to Agatha today?"

"If you mean ignoring her while she said mean stuff about me, yes," P said.

"That you need to give up on soccer?"

She paused. "Yeah. Pretty much."

"Good."

"Good?" she said, frowning.

Reggie nodded and went to wash his bowl. "Yeah. Good. I'll see you after the game."

"You sure you're feeling okay?"

"Yeah," Reggie said quietly. "I am."

That evening, Reggie stood alone in a pristine locker room. They had traveled to Milton in their usual run-down bus, gradually feeling the roads smooth beneath the tires, the land stretch into green, and the suburbs of the wealthier regions blossom around them like a huge stone garden. Though they had attended many away games, the team was still glued to the windows, amazed at the wealth that lived outside the Bottom. Reggie lay his head against the glass and watched it roll by, his mind elsewhere, his entire body primed and waiting for the big game.

And, beneath that, nervousness. Fear of failure. He realized he would not be able to banish it entirely before tonight. Maybe it would always be there—the little tingle of doubt. But he needed to play through it. He needed to rise above it. If he didn't, his grana would reflect his fear.

"Five minutes," the bus driver called from the front.

Twig glanced at Reggie. "This is it."

"You ready?"

Twig pretended to box the seat in front of him. "Ready as ever. Going to be a tough one."

"Sounds about right for the West Bottom Badgers," Reggie said.

Twig grinned. "My thoughts exactly."

The bus pulled to a stop, and the Badgers walked out in front of a beautiful steel-and-glass gym. Trees lined the entryway. New cars filled the parking lot. Reggie didn't care today. He just filed into the gym with his team, all under the condescending eyes of the lucky people born outside of the Bottom. He heard the jeers and comments. The cruel laughter. Reggie ignored that too. His fight was on the court. That was his entire world for the next two hours.

They gathered in the locker room, and Rolabi looked out over the team.

"You know what to do. All that matters now is who wants it more."

The team cheered, letting "Badgers!" ring through the cavernous space, and then streamed out.

Reggie turned to the door, taking another deep breath.

It was time.

17

THE GAME

When someone chases their dream, watch closely. Their effort
will throw off sparks, and perhaps your kindling is waiting.

✧ WIZENARD ⟨62⟩ PROVERB ✧

REGGIE CLOSED HIS eyes for a moment and listened to the sounds of anticipation. Cheers from the hometown Marauders fans. Shouts from both sets of players. The first whistle like the shriek of an eagle, calling the West Bottom Badgers onto the court. And his heartbeat below it all, thudding methodically, gaining speed.

The Milton Marauders were already taking their spots on the floor, waiting with predatory grins. They wore all-black jerseys with a red swashbuckling sword for a logo, layered over matching black T-shirts. Every player was oversize for his position. These were the conference's top recruits, and Oren Laithe stood at their center—six foot two, broad shoulders, ripple fade, and a scar that passed through the right side of his lips and deepened when he smiled. That smile was not so much taunting as deeply assured, like he was looking down from far above at whatever creatures had emerged from the Bottom and readying his boot.

Reggie felt that little spot of anxious fear growing in his belly, and he reminded himself that it didn't matter who he was playing tonight . . . as long as it wasn't himself.

Reggie lined up across from his check—a rangy, skilled shooting guard he remembered from last season. They called him Jay Day, since he rarely missed a jump shot. Jay Day turned when he saw Reggie get into position, and then looked him up and down with obvious disdain.

"I don't even have to guard Rain today?" he said. "Man . . . I was hoping for a little sweat."

"Sorry to disappoint you," Reggie murmured.

"Ready?" the head ref asked, stepping in for the jump ball.

"Of course," Oren said, lining up across from Twig. "Let's get this over with."

The ref threw the ball up, but Oren was a touch late. Twig won the tip, and the Badgers launched immediately into the Spotlight Offense with Rain at the top, calling out the first play.

"Six!"

Reggie got to his spot on the wing. Time seemed to have sped up again. The crowd and the squeaking shoes and his own pounding heart over it all. But today, he kept breathing. In and out. Stoking the fire. He had to be realistic. He knew he wasn't able to jump higher today. He wasn't faster or smarter or more skilled than he was yesterday. Today, the only change was that he was going to play the Marauders . . . not himself. But maybe, just maybe, that evened the odds.

Down low, a double screen played out. Lab used Cash as a

lumbering diversion and caught the ball on a back cut, laying it in for a quick two-point lead. The crowd quieted, clearly surprised even at that small victory, and he heard the Badgers cheering from the bench. Peño was shouting a battle cry. Reggie allowed a grin . . . but the rest of the quarter wasn't nearly as positive.

There were hard fouls. Constant smothering defense. Insults. But most alarmingly, the Marauders began to pull away. They were fast. They were strong. And Oren was dominant.

He looked like he was twelve going on twenty—only Cash could match him physically. The problem was that Cash was slow on the lateral step, and Oren put up twelve points early in the first quarter . . . including three mammoth dunks, which was a rare occurrence in Elite Youth League ball.

Every time, the gym exploded with noise.

Reggie was starting slow, but efficiently. He kept Jay Day in check and managed to knock down a few mid-range jumpers of his own, all from spots he usually avoided. He'd made about five thousand of them in the last few weeks, so it was starting to feel pretty comfortable. But his baskets were not nearly enough, and the Badgers were slipping fast.

As usual, Rain was playing inspired ball—this time facilitating the game with lightning-quick passes and hard drives—but he needed help. Soon.

"Come on, Cash," Rain urged as the Marauders attacked again. "Keep him out."

Oren had the ball on the far wing, and Cash was tentatively approaching him, eyes flicking around for screens. But Reggie knew that wasn't the game plan—Oren wanted Cash one-on-

one. Oren was too fast for him. And right on cue, the Marauders' center cleared the lane.

"Force him to the corner!" Reggie called. "Stay on your toes, big man!"

Oren took a step, and Cash lunged, trying to strip the ball. It was a poor choice. Oren immediately went the other way, dribbling with his stronger right hand, and then threw down yet another thunderous dunk. The crowd erupted. His teammates chest-bumped back down the court.

It felt like a blowout. He could sense the fans' hunger in the air, like a pot about to boil.

We can't lose, he reminded himself. *Not one more.*

The Badgers attacked again, and Rain took it hard to the rim. But the Marauders were starting to figure their game plan out. They collapsed both their forwards at once, squeezing Rain between them, and Oren swatted the ball away with a vicious volleyball spike, eliciting more cheers.

When the first quarter ended, the Badgers were down six. They were down by ten two minutes into the second. Then twelve. Things were starting to slip fast. The pot was boiling now.

Reggie kept playing hard, confident, and controlled. He was five for seven, and Jay Day only had three points. It wasn't enough.

Once in a while, Reggie saw a flicker of red around his teammates: Rain would suddenly look around for players, as if lost. The hoop would shrink for Cash. At one point, it seemed the entire court tilted toward the Badgers, letting the Marauders sprint easily downhill. As usual, no one else seemed to notice anything, but Reggie was sure they were moving faster.

It was clear that the Badgers were afraid . . . and in their fear, they were projecting negative grana. He knew what that meant. They were slipping into a hole, and they would have a hard time crawling back out. Reggie hit a corner three the next play—a once-unthinkable shot—but the Marauders came right back down the court, attacking Cash one-on-one again.

The score slipped further and further. So did the season. So did everything.

When the first half ended, the Badgers shuffled into the locker room. They were down by fifteen points, and on the other side of the gym, the Marauders were already celebrating. Reggie suspected they would pull their starters early in the third quarter if this continued. Oren would probably put his feet up and shout at the Badgers to go back to the Bottom where they belonged.

Reggie knew he was playing well. It was his best game as a Badger, to be sure: thirteen points, three assists, and five rebounds. And they were still getting beaten. He needed more.

He needed to find another level.

"You got to roll faster," Peño was telling Cash, using his hands to illustrate. "I can see it every time from the bench. You need to fight down there. Get physical. Wear Oren down."

The team was gathered in the locker room now, and they were clearly frustrated.

"I'm getting pinned," Cash said. "The center is picking me every time."

Lab hunched over, hands on his knees. "You all need to find me in the corner."

"You're covered," Vin snapped. "You need to get free—"

"All of you have to get back on defense," Big John said. "We're getting killed on—"

"*Enough.*"

Rolabi's voice cracked through the chatter like a whip as he stalked inside.

"We all know how to play," Rolabi said. "We prepared. We created a game plan."

"It isn't working—" Lab started.

"Because you have decided to lose," Rolabi replied. "You have accepted defeat."

Reggie looked around the room. Slouched shoulders and downcast eyes. It was true.

They were all ready to lose again. To bid goodbye to another season. To *bend*.

"Do not focus on the score," Rolabi continued. "Just win every moment from here on out."

"They are too good—" Jerome started.

Rolabi rounded on him. His eyes were blue green, flashing, and Jerome shrank back.

"Then we beat them by working harder. Reggie, I want you on Oren on defense. Man defense . . . no matter what everyone else is playing. I want this lead in single digits by the fourth."

Reggie nodded. He was giving up two inches and maybe forty pounds in that matchup. He was outmatched in size, strength, and probably even skill. But Reggie said nothing. He had said time and time again that he wanted to earn this, and now it was time to back it up. His goal right now was to shut Oren down. As the team started out again, Rain grabbed him and held him back.

"Remember when you knocked me on my butt? And then Jerome?"

"Yeah . . ." Reggie said.

"We need *that* Reggie. The one who refused to let one more person score on him."

"Right."

"Not one more loss," Rain said. "Keep Oren contained. Let's take this home."

They exchanged props and walked out onto the floor together.

The whistle went, and the Marauders attacked again. As soon as they crossed the halfway line, Reggie went to meet Oren, sticking to him every step of the way, his every muscle primed.

"Bit scrawny for a power forward," Oren said, smirking. "You sure about this?"

Reggie ignored him, racking his brain for ideas. Reggie was outsized and outgunned, so he had to play smarter. He needed to block the driving lanes and either force Oren to his weaker left hand or, better yet, challenge him to shoot from distance. Oren was a killer in the paint, but he was not a confident long-range shooter. If they were going to win, he had to make Oren shoot.

"Call for help if you need it!" Lab shouted.

Reggie could translate that easily enough: *You are going to need help.*

"Will do," he said wryly.

The Marauders attacked, fanning out and sending their center deep like the tip of an arrow. Oren got to the top of the key, putting his hand up and sending a dismissive elbow right into Reggie's solar plexus. Reggie gasped and stumbled back, but he was used to taking cheap shots. He didn't look at the ref. He didn't complain. He just got into his stance, focusing on his footwork and keeping a hand on Oren's back, tilting to block his opponent's stronger right side.

Oren got the ball high, and Reggie instantly fell back a foot or two, giving him plenty of space to turn. Oren faced him, keeping the ball high and wearing that same cocky, lopsided grin.

He faked the three, but Reggie didn't even flinch.

Go ahead, he thought. *Shoot it.*

Oren tried to go right, but Reggie slid in his way, still keeping his space—primed on his toes, back straight, arms out to block the lanes. No overreactions. No reaching. And after two more futile fakes, Oren finally rose up and took the deep three. It clanked off the rim.

Twig grabbed the rebound, and Reggie sprinted up the floor. One defensive stand down.

Probably fifty to go, he reminded himself.

"See the court, Reggie," Rolabi called, his voice cutting over the noise. "Adapt to it."

Reggie glanced at him. He was right: they needed to be smarter on offense. Rain was playing well, but he was getting frustrated, and the Marauders had figured out their approach.

As Reggie got to his spot, his eyes swept over the defense. It was a 2-3 zone: two guards up top, the center in the middle, and the forwards stretching out on either side of him, ready to step out on the corner threes. Reggie had already noted that their center was aggressive—he always wanted to attack the ball and block it if it went anywhere near the paint. Getting him out of the way *could* create a hole.

"Run an eight," Reggie shouted to Rain.

Rain nodded. "Eight!"

Reggie cut to the top of the key. It was open, of course—the two guards had to spread themselves to block the passes to either wing, and there was a nice little bubble of space where Reggie caught the ball. He turned, pretending to shoot, and the center came flying out at him, clearly trying to swat the ball into the stratosphere. For a second, it seemed so *slow*. So obvious.

Reggie faked the shot, saw Twig left open on the block, and hit him with an easy bounce pass for the layup. Things sped up again as Reggie ran back, but when he settled into a man defense, he began to analyze the attack in the same way, watching as Oren took his spot. The Marauders liked to run high screens and set up lobs to their post players. It was a good strategy—the Badgers' guards got stranded on the perimeter, and Twig and Cash were isolated.

But as Oren ran to set a screen, Reggie lagged for just a moment, watching the point guard's eyes. Twig was down low against their center, jockeying for position, and the point guard threw the pass. Their center caught the ball, brought it down to prepare for a turnaround jumper . . . and was instantly stripped.

Reggie had followed the ball like a bloodhound and ripped it free.

He put it on the floor, dribbling out of pressure, and then hit Rain on the outlet pass. Rain laid it in uncontested. Reggie didn't even smile. There was no time to celebrate. Back to work.

There was shoving and talking and fouling. Reggie took elbows to the ribs and chin. He spaced the floor on offense, shooting from all over the court. He didn't hit them all, but he hit enough, and Oren was forced to track him everywhere. Whenever Oren slacked to help in the paint, Reggie hit jumpers. When Oren attacked too quickly, Reggie faked and blew past him.

On defense, Reggie just let him shoot, always just far enough away from the hoop that he was likely to miss. The Badgers edged closer. Down six. Four. Two.

Reggie could barely think. He was working so hard, it was all just muscle memory now—a sort of rhythmic, unconscious movement that took over his limbs. His eyes burned. His sides ached. And with thirty seconds to go, the Milton Marauders had the ball.

As the Marauders dribbled down the floor, Reggie mapped out how the play would go. If they were focused on killing time, then they weren't thinking about playing for the best shot. That was a plus. The Badgers were down only one, and if the Marauders missed, there would be six seconds left with the chance for a last-shot comeback win. They needed to trust their defense.

"Nothing easy!" Reggie shouted. "Play to the last second!"

The Badgers defended stubbornly, blocking the lanes. The Marauders moved the ball around the top of the circle, trying to waste time. When the shot clock dropped to 4 . . . 3 . . . 2 . . . their point guard put up a desperate, fading three-pointer.

It clanked off the rim, and Reggie secured the rebound, wrapping it up protectively.

"Time!" Rolabi called on cue.

Reggie checked the clock as he ran in to join the huddle. Five seconds to go, and they could advance the ball to the other half. That was more than enough time to get an open look.

Reggie glanced at Rain, expecting to see the star guard pumping himself up.

But Rain was looking at him. Everyone was.

"We're going to set a simple screen," Rolabi said. "Rain and Lab will be decoys at the top of the key. Reggie, run the baseline off a screen from Twig. Go to the corner. Take the shot."

"Your shot, bro," Rain said to Reggie.

"You got this," Twig added. "Go wizenard these jerks."

Rolabi glanced at Twig, raising an eyebrow, but said nothing.

Reggie was surprised, but he managed a nod. He supposed he hadn't really been thinking about it, but he had been shooting a lot. He didn't even know how many points he had anymore, but it was well over thirty, and many of them had come in the fourth quarter. He had the hot hand, and Rolabi always played to the moment. He felt his guts clench with nervous energy.

"Just like you've been practicing," Rolabi said knowingly.

"Yes, sir."

Reggie walked onto the court, trying to drown out all the cheers and shouting.

"Coming for the screen," Twig said quietly, nodding at him. "You got this, Reggie."

"I'll be ready."

Cash had the inbound, so Rain, Reggie, and Lab clumped together. Time seemed to slow down again. Reggie could barely hear anything other than the rhythmic thudding of his own heart. Lab was talking, but it was interrupted by the beat: "Get to"—*boom*—"and we'll"—*boom*.

The whistle blew, and Twig stepped up from the block, setting a pick. Reggie rubbed off his shoulder just as Rain and Lab broke in either direction like loosed arrows. Reggie stepped through into space, catching the hard inbound from Cash and turning to the hoop, taking a glance up at the shot clock above the hoop. From somewhere far away, he heard the crowd counting:

"Five . . . four . . ."

Oren was rushing at him, so he dribbled right past him before Oren could slow his momentum. Reggie rounded the top of the arc and took a step inside. The best shot available.

"Three . . . two . . ."

Reggie rose up. Everything slowed. He kept his elbow pointed at the rim. Feet together. Fingers rolling along the pebbling until the ball flew, wrist following, everything aimed at destiny.

"One . . ."

Reggie felt something collide with his shoulder. He twisted in midair, throwing a wild shot, and then hit the floor. A whistle pierced the air, cutting over the drone of the final buzzer. Reggie lay there, dazed. It was a shooting foul. He had two free throws to win the game.

Rain and Twig hauled him up, both clapping his shoulders as he headed to the line. He barely heard what they were saying. It seemed like the whole gym had gone quiet. Reggie stood on the free-throw line and breathed deeply, trying to catch his breath. There was no time left on the clock. If he hit these shots, the game was over. The Badgers would win their first away game ever.

They would beat the conference champions. Maybe, just maybe, they would start a run.

The ref passed him the ball, and he dribbled twice, still breathing deeply. He hit the first.

The noise rushed back in. The crowd was cheering. His teammates were pumping their fists. One more, and they were there. Reggie caught the ball, smiling. His story had been written.

He took three dribbles, one more deep breath, and took the shot. It spiraled toward history . . . and then it hit the back iron, bounced once more off the rim, and dropped to the floor.

The Marauders cheered. His teammates slumped.

Reggie watched the ball roll away, incredulous. He had missed.

He'd had his big, triumphant moment that he had worked so hard for, and he'd *missed*.

Disappointment and anger and guilt flooded through him. His knees buckled.

"Two-minute break," the referee said over the noise. "Then we have overtime."

18

THE TURN

When we feel entitled to victory, we no longer deserve it.

✦ WIZENARD ⟨63⟩ PROVERB ✦

REGGIE SAT ON the bench among his teammates as the clock counted down the two-minute break, barely listening to the chatter around him, replaying the free throw in his mind again and again. He could see the slow spiral of the ball. It had looked so perfect . . . but it wasn't. It never was for him. He had clawed and fought so hard for that chance at glory, and he'd missed it.

Vaguely, he still knew overtime was coming. He knew he had to focus, but it seemed like all the air had gone out of him. It felt like his dreams and destiny and perfect story had all clanked off the iron and fallen away. He could imagine P's disappointment.

Twig slid closer to him, patting his knee. "You ready to go again, man?"

"Yeah," he murmured. "Sure."

"Nobody blames you for missing that shot. You know that, right?" Twig said.

"I do."

Twig frowned. "You tied the game, dude. We're in OT. This is it."

"I had the win on my fingertips—"

"Yeah. And the shot missed. So what?"

"*So what?*" Reggie asked. "That was it. A chance to turn it around—"

Twig shook his head. "It wasn't enough anyway. We need more."

Reggie flushed, feeling his temper rise. "I was working hard—"

"You were. It was an amazing game. We hung in there, and we fought, and we had a chance to win. That's all great. But even if we win this one, it's gonna get harder. We need more."

Twig grabbed Reggie's shoulder and gave him a shake.

"Man, we watched you in practice for years. You probably didn't even see it. You can dominate. It came and went, but lately, it's just crazy. You're unstoppable, dude. Don't worry about the playoffs right now. Talin, grana, anything. Focus. Don't let them get another point."

"It's just that you work, and you get there, and you miss—"

"You got to keep earning it," Twig said. "It doesn't matter what you did yesterday or this morning or five minutes ago. Go earn it right now. Pick this team up and let it all out, man. I know you have more. We all do. Forget the playoffs and the Bottom and all of that. Just go *ball.*"

Reggie looked down at his hands. He thought he'd won ball over. That he had worked hard enough to earn the love of the game. That the tide had turned, and they were winning, and he would never have to struggle again. But maybe it wasn't a onetime deal. Maybe he had to *keep* working to deserve it.

He'd forgotten something—it wasn't the destination he loved. It was the little moments. The feel of the game.

He loved to ball, and *that* was what he worked for.

He sat back, feeling the doubt seep out of him. All the concerns about what he had to prove, and what this meant . . . he let it all go.

"Not one more point," he whispered.

"It's time," Rolabi said.

Reggie stood up, hands balled into fists, eyes narrowed. Fresh energy coursed through him. He saw green lines tracing through the room, pulsing with his heartbeat. His mind was locked on winning. Not the season. Not even the game. The next possession. The next *second*.

His entire body trembled. It felt like he was on fire.

Twig stood up beside him. "Reggie?"

"Let's go," Reggie whispered. "Like Rolabi said . . . it's time."

He strode onto the court as the clock moved to zero.

"Forget the cheering," Reggie called over his shoulder. "We've got a game to win."

"What did you say to him?" he overheard Rain ask.

"I don't know," Twig said. "But I'm glad I'm on his team right now."

Reggie crouched low, waiting for the tip. His breath rose and fell. The whole gym pumped with his lungs. He felt the floor tilting toward the far net. He saw the hoop widen. He heard no cheers. Saw no crowds. There was only the ball and two hoops.

The ball went up, Twig won the tip, and it came to Reggie. He caught it, feeling another surge of energy. The Marauders were scrambling into position. They seemed slow, disorganized. Maybe he was moving too fast. Whatever it was, he attacked.

Reggie raced down the floor, weaved through the defenders, and laid it into a Hula-Hoop rim with ease. There were no pumped fists. No smiles. He ran back and stripped the ball the second it touched his defender. Then he scored again. And again. The floor tilted so far, he felt like he was flying down the court. The hoop was so big, he could drain shots from anywhere.

No one could touch him.

It was complete domination in the end. Fourteen straight points in overtime, and zero allowed. Reggie had scored every point. Threes, layups, free throws. When the buzzer went, he just stood there while his teammates went mad. They had beaten the best team in the conference in an away game. It was history.

Reggie relished the *feel* of it. The feel of having worked, and won, and earned it.

Rain and Twig enveloped him, chanting "Badgers," and then the rest followed, and he let himself be swept into the celebrations. But just for a little while. They had a lot more work to do.

Reggie could hardly wait.

19

INTO THE STORM

The mountain will never bend to the storm.

❖ WIZENARD ⑦⓪ PROVERB ❖

SIX WEEKS LATER, Reggie slid into the front seat of Gran's car in Fairwood's parking lot, wiping the last vestiges of sweat from his face. Gran and P had insisted on waiting for Reggie at the end of the game, even though the team's celebrations had taken nearly an hour. Rolabi had allowed the Badgers to cut down one of the nets and take a piece each to remember their historic regular season, since they wouldn't play a game in Fairwood again until next year.

Rolabi did pointedly remind them there was much left to be done, but even he cracked a smile when they all hoisted Peño up. Reggie clutched his piece in his hand now, still amazed that they had actually done it: the West Bottom Badgers were heading to the nationals.

They had needed seven straight wins, and tonight, in their final game of the season, they had beaten the Bears by twenty points. In two weeks, they would be leaving for Argen.

"Well, that was something," P said from the back seat.

Reggie watched the city roll by, still wearing a big smile. "Yeah."

"I think there is a sale at Bennett's," Gran said suddenly.

Reggie glanced at her. "What?"

"Forty percent, I think. Closing sale, apparently, but they always claim they're closing."

P leaned forward, frowning. "Gran, what does a clothing store have to do with anything?"

"Well, Reginald is going to need a new outfit if he's going to Argen. Something clean."

Reggie laughed, and P joined in. Even Gran cracked a smile, and then told them to stop distracting her or they all could get out and walk . . . even the "big-shot basketball player."

Reggie rolled the white netting around in his fingers, savoring the feeling. It was more than a piece of string to him—it represented the entire year, and the struggle through self-doubt to become the player he was meant to be. And it was a reminder that there was more to come.

P smiled. "What do you think Mom and Dad would say if they could see us right now?"

Gran glanced at her in the rearview mirror. "I think they would say: Patricia, please listen to your gran."

"Or maybe: Reggie, take a shower," P added, sniffing the air.

"All right, we're done here," Reggie said.

P tapped her chin. "Or maybe: Reggie, you should give P your bedroom—"

"That's enough for today," Rolabi said.

The team broke apart from their drill, some hunching over from exhaustion, others sharing props and slapped shoulders for getting through another tough practice. They had all been hard, of course, but now, in the weeks leading up to the nationals, they were grueling.

Reggie and Twig sat down together on the bench, both sopping wet.

"Man, I hope I live to see Argen," Twig groaned, stretching out his legs.

"We don't just want to see it. We want to get there and win."

Twig snorted. "Between you and Rolabi, I think we'll be ready."

Rolabi had packed up for the day, but he was standing at center court, waiting.

"Do you think we'll get a better bus for the drive there?" Twig asked. "It's like a thirty-hour drive, and we don't have a bathroom, TVs . . . reliable tires . . ."

"I doubt it. Bring a book."

"And a bucket," Twig muttered. "Well, it doesn't matter. I can't wait."

Reggie grinned. "Me either."

Twig stood up, gave Reggie props, and started out. "You know," he called over his shoulder, "if we win, it's going to be kind of hard to call this place the Bottom, right?"

Reggie laughed. He lingered on the bench, taking his time to change his shoes, until all the others had gone. Rolabi was still standing there. Reggie slid his bag over his shoulder and approached his coach.

"It was quite the season for you," Rolabi said.

Reggie swallowed. Coming from Rolabi, this was high praise.

"Not over yet," Reggie managed.

"No. The big teams are waiting."

Reggie nodded. "We'll be ready."

"Good. The whole team must believe we can compete, even dominate, at the national level. They must feel it in their bones, or we have no chance."

"So . . . you want me to tell the guys we can actually do this?"

"I want you to *show them*. You have a special role on this team, Reggie."

"What's that?"

Rolabi allowed a rare smile. "I just told you. And your mother knew it too."

"My mother—" he said, heat rushing to his cheeks.

"Why do you leave someone an empty box?" Rolabi asked.

"Well . . . I don't know. Because you want them to fill it, maybe."

"Exactly. And I trust you to fill it wisely."

"Did you know my parents?" Reggie asked, almost desperately.

"No. But I know of them. And I know they would be proud."

Rolabi patted Reggie's shoulder and started for the door.

"They raised a good son. He alone must choose if he will become *great*."

"Is that why you were so hard on me?" Reggie called after him. "To motivate me?"

"My job is to bring out the best from everyone. For some, facing your fear is the way to improvement. For others, it is winning a battle against the limitations we impose on ourselves."

He opened the door, then turned back. "Ah . . . and, Reggie?"

"Yes?"

"Luckily, that particular battle doesn't end. It means we can *never* stop improving."

Reggie nodded. "I understand."

"Good. Now let's go show the world the Bottom is back."

When Reggie got home, P was lying in her bedroom, rereading one of the books from her small collection.

"Any good?" Reggie asked.

She lowered it. "As good as the last twenty times. Can I come to Argen?"

He laughed. She had been asking that since the day they'd won. But it would be too expensive for Gran and P to travel to the capital on their own, and the bus had no space for players' families.

"Fine. I don't need you to take me. Maybe I'll go somewhere on my own."

Reggie smiled. "Maybe so. Let's play our game."

P sat up, grinning. "You never want to play anymore."

"Today, I do."

"You want to go first?" she asked.

"Second."

She snorted. "The—"

"Girl—"

"Named—"

"P—" he said.

P laughed. "Is—"

"Going—"

"To—" she said.

"Be *anything* she wants. Even if she can be a real pain in the butt sometimes."

P frowned. "I don't think you remember the rules."

"Maybe not. But I like the ending. And you said that was the important part."

She giggled. "I guess."

"Good night, P," Reggie said, heading to his bedroom.

There was something he wanted to do.

Rolabi had reminded him.

He walked into his room, closed the door, and took the old box off the dresser. Sitting down on his bed, he ran his hands over the cover and the intricate carved symbol.

"I don't know what the note means. I don't really understand this symbol, or grana. I don't know where this sport I love is going to lead me. But if I'm going to fill this box with something, it might as well be a reminder that I will never quit."

He grabbed the little piece of mesh from his dresser and laid it inside.

For a moment, it seemed as if the symbol on the lid shone with a pure, emerald green.

He sat back and smiled. It was the end of the regular season, but it felt like a beginning.

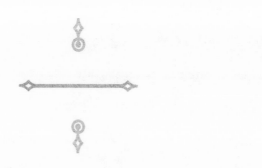

WIZENARD PROVERBS

When the road grows hard, and your legs tire, know that greatness lies ahead.

The world is not always ready when you are. It rewards only those who stay ready.

If you are fully present in every moment, time will be your ally.

The one who works without boasting has twice the time to improve. Beware the quiet contenders.

Every human is born to change the world. Unfortunately, some are changed by the world first.

All people are magnets. They simply must choose to push or pull.

Train your mind in conjunction with your body, or both will fail.

Compromise is a part of life. But not when it comes to dreams. For those, one must seek the stars or nothing.

Self-doubt is the beginning of defeat.

We are not inspired by success. We are inspired by the triumph over adversity.

The defeated look at the night sky and see their own insignificance. The dreamer sees their potential.

When someone chases their dream, watch closely. Their effort will throw off sparks, and perhaps your kindling is waiting.

When we feel entitled to victory, we no longer deserve it.

Before asking when, tell yourself how.

A champion turns weakness into strength.

Your mind is a filter; when it is clouded, you cannot see the light.

Talent is a seed. To flourish, it must be watered with sweat.

The deeper the hole, the longer the climb, and the stronger you arrive.

Struggle is the training of the soul.

The mountain will never bend to the storm.

KOBE BRYANT is an Academy Award winner, a *New York Times* best-selling author, and the CEO of Granity Studios, a multimedia content creation company. He spends every day focused on creating stories that inspire the next generation of athletes to be the best versions of themselves. In a previous life, Kobe was a five-time NBA champion, two-time NBA Finals MVP, NBA MVP, and two-time Olympic gold medalist. He hopes to share what he's learned with young athletes around the world.

***

WESLEY KING is the *New York Times* best-selling author of eleven novels, including *The Wizenard Series: Training Camp*, *OCDaniel*, the Vindico series, and *A World Below*. His books have been optioned for film and television and translated for release worldwide. Besides writing, he is working on a circumnavigation on a 1967 sailboat. You can follow him on Instagram @wesleykingauthor or on Twitter @WesleyTKing.

GRANITY STUDIOS, LLC
GRANITYSTUDIOS.COM

Library of Congress Control Number: 2019954885
ISBN (hardcover): 9781949520149
ISBN (eBook): 9781949520156

Printed in the United States of America
1 3 5 7 9 10 8 6 4 2

Book design by Karina Granda
Cover and interior art by Spandana Myneni
Cover lettering by Melanie Lapovich
Endpaper art by Shahab Alizadeh